Eventually,

EMMA LAIRD

ISBN: 9781793429933

A Note From The Writer

I started writing this book in a coffee shop below my apartment in Crystal Palace, around May 2018. I had no idea that it would turn into a book. In fact, I'm surprised it even escaped from the notes section on my laptop, where many other sporadic hours of typing never made it past chapter one. It started with Bryce. I wanted to write about my personal experiences, about the emotions I was feeling, without actually thinking about my own life. I wanted to write about being in love and having a seemingly perfect life that could so easily turn to turmoil. So I fuelled all of my real emotions into a fictional plot. It became therapeutic for me. So much so that I can't imagine my life without writing now.

This book is confusing for me, it's been a long process of self-doubt and has always seemed somewhat messy. Not because I've embedded some of my own life into the storyline, but because I've used such different experiences with different people, and merged them into one narrative. From a car journey with a friend to a moment in a relationship, a first kiss, or simply just moments like an overheard conversation, or a late night chat with a friend that stuck in my mind. They were then manipulated, twisted, or heightened into Kora's world - maybe into a way in which I wished they'd have panned out in real life. And then more ideas would flood to me, the picture would become clearer, and then *eventually* it was just a case of piecing the puzzle together.

So I guess writing like that, distorting so much of myself, led me to question whether what I was writing was *right.*

Despite Bryce, more than any other character, being attached to so much of myself, I see him not as somebody I know, but somebody I have created. He is a stranger to me, he doesn't remind me of anybody from my personal life - in fact, I wish Bryce existed. I'm proud of him the most, I think. He is an elusive mixture of failed relationships, of people I have met only for one night or even memories of someone I've held a gaze with from across the room, and have never seen since. I feel slightly shielded in knowing that *Eventually,* is ultimately, fiction. These characters aren't real and Kora certainly is not how I see myself.

But it's been confusing none the less, trying to figure out how to get this world in my head into words on a page. How to mix real life with fiction and make it all just *fit.* I hope I have finally figured it out. Maybe I should have written a biography instead, that way I would have known its authenticity. But in the end, this is what we're left with: what you're holding in your hands now. I hope you don't think as cynically of my work as I do.

Contents

Eventually,

Acknowledgements

When I was younger, maybe seven or eight, my mum took me to drama classes. I loved it so much I insisted on going even when unwell, which resulted in being sick all over my mum's car - and my mum never taking me back. To any parents reading: allowing your child creative freedom, in whatever way that may be, is more valuable than you may think. Let them dance and scribble and explore their creativity because in those few classes I did go to, I discovered what I wanted to do for the rest of my life. Sending your child into the big wide world with big dreams is scary, but sending them with none at all is all the more scarier, I think.

So I guess my first acknowledgement is to my *mum*. Thanks for letting me throw up in your car.

Secondly to *Liam*, who's selflessness and honestly has allowed me the comfort to explore my own boundaries with writing. Who has so often sat with me in coffee shops or let me stay for hours eating his food while we edited these very words. He helped me create some beautiful moments in this book. He even came up with Bryce's last name which I think is very special; almost as if a part of him is soaring through these very pages.

To him, I will be forever grateful for his belief and our friendship which allows us both to put forward the most absurd of ideas without judgement and receive nothing but honesty in return. This book truly wouldn't exist without him.

To *Chris*, for staying up late with me, talking about anything and everything, opposing my opinions simply to test my knowledge - I think in those chats alone, I was left with another perspective, a new way of thinking, seeing things in more than one way (which has proved very useful in writing). You've taught me many things in life, shared with me films and music that have had nearly as big of an influence on my life as you have done yourself. Words can't really describe what you mean to me. So, thanks for being smart.

To my *dad*. Who my love for nature truly attributes to. My fondest memories as a child were those spent with you in the Peak District. This book is surely a testament of that. Thank you.

To my old *school library*, where I once was fined £20 for writing on a table. But more importantly, where I spent so many of my lunch breaks reading books I'd randomly plucked from shelves. Where my love for reading flourished.

To *Models 1* who have truly been like a second family to me. I love them with all of my heart and this book is just another expression that they've allowed me to release. To *Ouarda,* thanks for believing in me and pushing me with my projects, to *Jess, Chanel,* to *Ezzie,* my dearest *Uwe* and especially to *Joe.* You reminded me that I was always Emma before I was a model. Thank you all for your endless support and belief.

To *the loves of my life and the ones that have come close.* The ones who infatuated me with just a look, confused me, even the ones that hurt me. Thank you for allowing me to *feel.* To appreciate the smaller things we so often overlook, and enabling the need to externalise my emotions into this book.

To *Wilde, Fitzgerald, Rowling, Dali,* to name a few of those who influenced me throughout my childhood. For giving me escapism and a fascination that seemed so otherworldly when I was a child, which I hope this book can create at least a fraction of for others.

And finally, of course, the music. The *bloody* music. There is an unintentional theme of that throughout the story. The bands deserve a mention for being such a big part of my life, whether it be an accompaniment on my drives from Derbyshire to London, or their sounds penetrating my house through my amplifier while I dance on my own, or cry, or laugh. Regardless, the music is always there. So a thank you to the ones that made it into the book in some way or another: *Joy Disivion, Lana Del Rey, The Kooks, Arctic Monkeys, Lorde, Kasabian, Reverend & The Makers, The Smiths, The Wombats, Razorlight, Etta James, Queen, The Kooks, The Pigeon Detectives, Muse, The Killers, AC/DC, The Strokes, Leonard Cohen, David Bowie.*

This book is for anybody who wants to escape.

Eventually,

part one
the break up

Eventually,

Tiredness is heavy on my eyes
my legs on your thighs
and eyes open wide
fighting the light
to be here with you
relishing
an infatuation in growth
it began like so…

The Silence Of The Lambs

I woke late, unlike me. Early mornings graced me with beautiful sunrises and songs from birds, but would always be compromised for late nights with Bryce. And last night was another compromise worth making.

The titles rolled. I switched the TV off and looked to him. His hair had started sprouting grey in its fringe, and I loved it. I reached my fingers from under the blanket to stroke through his curls. I was close enough to lean in for a kiss but resisted. Just to look at him was all I wanted for now. My touch was met with a smile at the corner of his mouth, his top lip thinning, hiding his teeth. I'm sure he knew what that smile did to me. After two years, the same effect. It encouraged my body closer as he stared at me, anticipating what my next move might be. With my eyes still on his, I placed my hands on his thigh, weaving through the rips of his jeans, only to stop at his knee which sat nicely in my palm.

Again he smirked and lifted himself from the sofa. I felt the cold as he left me exposed, the blanket half on the floor. It was late November, and I suppose living in an old church had its disadvantages in the colder months. The fire had ebbed away without our notice at some point during our favourite film, *The Silence Of The Lambs.*

"Do you want some drink in this?" he called from the kitchen, the kettle whistling from the stove.

"That could be dangerous," I smirked.

He came in with two steaming cups and placed them on the wooden table in front of us, where my feet had happily been perched. I could smell the alcohol overpowering, and smiled at the thoughts of the last night we did this. He sat closer to me this time, buried his head and exhaled a sigh into my chest. He then sat up to trace his fingers, still hot from the cups, along my bare arms, up to my shoulders and over the thin spaghetti straps of my vest. He lifted both in unison and dropped them from my shoulders where they landed just above my elbows. I had goose-bumps. Maybe from the cold, most likely from his touch.

"Our tea might go cold," I protested weakly, a whisper. That smirk again. He wasn't looking at me, but painting a picture over my skin with his fingers: over my collarbones, up my neck, around the curls of my hair and finally onto my face. They moved onto my lips that parted in obedience. Slowly my tongue moved over his thumb. Currents glugged down my back, his fingers driving them, revving and then stalling on the curves of my body where his hands would usually rest. I sat cradling him, my eyes locked on his.

—

What if
one day I wake up
and the bed is cold
if you become a memory
and I forget you
what if
the days now a norm
become scarce
a moment lost
something that maybe even
never was

—

I wanted this feeling to stay. I wanted to create this in my memory now because if I only ever had memories, I needed them to be of this; I made sure I took everything in. I closed my eyes and let each sensation, each emotion fill my mind. A lump formed in my throat that I quickly swallowed away.

—

Soon my scent will seep over yours
so I will wear your shirt and dread the day
I might forget the colour of your eyes
or the tones in your voice
and your touch will feel less real
I will be like everybody else
an outsider
I will see you on the tv
and wish that we could meet
as if we never really did
just like everybody else

—

"Are we going to bed?" He was confused at the thoughts that seeped from my expression.

"No." A faint whisper.

Happy with what I'd captured in my memory, I gently pushed him onto his back, still cradling him. He almost took up the length of the sofa and I saw small goosebumps raise the hairs on his arms as he touched the cold leather, where none of us had been sat. I smiled at him and innocently grabbed my tea. Way too much liquor. His expression told me it wasn't an accident. I winced as it went down my throat before my face threw him a half-hearted scold.

Eventually,

A Tradition

I'd grown up with a love for music. The paradoxical feeling of intimacy amongst thousands of people at music festivals in the summer, concerts in the winter, was what I lived for. In all of the rain and cold and dirt, we would camp in tents with wet sleeping bags and struggle more to find dry clothes buried beneath heaps of alcohol, cigarette packets, and instant noodles with each day that passed.

We would brush our teeth every morning under a running tap at the drinking station, where others quenched their thirst from a night of excessive drinking. That same tap would be the closest thing people got to a shower all weekend: though I'm not sure a few splashes against the face would ever constitute as one. The sounds of generators would surround us, coming from food stalls which sold hot drinks in styrofoam and bacon sandwiches wrapped in napkins. There would be a mixture of smells in the air, mostly doughnuts and weed.

I would laugh kindheartedly at the boys congregating under small gazebos, scattered around the campsite, well away from the family area. Where if you looked closely enough you would see the whites of their eyes disappearing just as fast as the drugs dissolving inside of them. Where teenage boys wore bucket hats and trainers instead of boots, whose feet were surely sodden with mud for the entirety of the weekend. And where smoke escaped then disappeared over the rain during that limbo stage of the day - between the early morning rise from the sun creeping through and heating your tent, and the afternoon music slots.

Under these gazebos you'd recollect yourself from the previous night, eat the food you'd heaved across the fields along with your camping chair, clothes and crates of beer on the day of arrival until you found a spot to pitch up.

If ever there was a time over these weekends that boys should be closer to hydration than dehydration, it were those spent under the gazebo: the only chance for rehabilitation, the calm before the chaos, and a rehearsal of songs they would later hear live as they struggled to amplify the field with a portable speaker and the occasional group of passing strangers joining the choir.

They embraced the rain with each drag of green, despite their failed attempts to find a girl each night. Invariably saddening were the opposing views Tilda had upon most things we talked of nowadays. Where I laughed as we walked past those boys, she scowled and made disheartening comments towards a group of strangers who she presumed to be beneath her. I smiled, safe in the knowledge that her judgement was unnoticed; their laughter untarnished by her pessimism.

Not even those constant smells of weed and doughnuts could overpower the stench of the portable toilets: the only thing me and Tilda equally detested.

Those festivals were always my favourite memories. Even fearing for our lives when someone decided to set fire to their tent on the last night. It all sat fondly in my mind. To then go back to the reality of daily showers, a comfortable bed and hydration was a bittersweet reality.

Though I'd left school many years before, Tilda and I had an unspoken pledge where we would reunite every summer for whatever festivals had the best acts, or whichever ones she could get free tickets to. Tilda was a journalist for a magazine, so press passes were not uncommon during the summer. This came with the luxury of private viewing areas, VIP access and the occasional backstage pass. We spent most of our time out in the field watching the bands, trying to recreate those childhood memories we'd made long ago, not really knowing we were creating a tradition. But we did start to prefer the intimacy of the VIP area for the fresher toilets and quieter bar, and secretly, the people watching.

—

A buzz of people
of music
dampness
and drunkenness
a love for it all
where we might moan
but wouldn't change a thing
where we would drink
but it would never erase
where we would be cold
but it would never lessen
our excitement when
the lights flickered colour
against fields scattered
with strangers
who came to love
drink
cry
fuck
and everything in-between

—

During one particular summer, I had two hoods from my multiple layers of clothing shielded around my face. I wore Doc Martins, barely visible beneath the mud and I'm pretty sure I had mascara seeping down my face because the weather rarely seemed to behave at festivals, at least in the UK. I was waiting for Tilda outside the toilets where a queue was quickly growing after The Kooks had finished playing. I looked around at the eccentrics and musicians around me. There was a group of two girls, three boys who'd squeezed onto a bench and who were singing along to distant bands on stage, drinking from plastic cups. One of the girls clenched her denim jacket around her waist as the wind blew a hard gust. I felt the cold too and was thankful for the extra pair of socks I was wearing. My eyes moved onto the next bench -

that's when we first saw each other.

He wore neatly ironed trousers, brown, with a fold down the middle of each leg and a black leather belt through the loopholes. Tucked beneath was an equally crisp white shirt with a large collar sitting perfectly to expose his dark curls of chest hair, and a thin gold chain around his neck. He seemed to be greeting the rain without a wince, out of place amongst the girls around us flocking to shelter. After allowing a little time to roll over his body, I stopped at his face. His eyes were the lightest shade of blue, a contrast to his dark brown hair and slight tan. He was stood with a group of boys who all seemed deep in conversation, though he was vacant, detached - looking at *me*. For a moment my heart stopped, the world too, and all my mind knew was him.

The sound of conversations surrounding me as people drunkenly stumbled through the mud in different directions, Tilda in the bathroom, the cold that was sprouting red blotches over my exposed neck, everything was forgotten while we looked at each other at that moment. I wished it could last forever. Smiles hovered around our mouths whilst we tried to communicate with silence, through distance. Nerves refrained me from making the first move and left me wondering what his voice sounded like - *was it how I imagined?* Did he have the personality to match his perfect exterior? I thought he did; it seemed to ooze from him, radiating through his smile. I bet he could attract anyone. I was sure most people wanted to be his friend and if they didn't, they were probably madly in love with him.

He was tall, but short enough to wrap my arms around his neck, if I were on the tips of my toes, and bury my head below his ear. I would feel his hands spread across and then hold my back. His touch would be everything to me, I'd live for it. He could make living feel like a dream: a constant state of high. My own drug. An addiction. And maybe he would be as addicted to me. That alone would feel like I was eating him up like a pill every day. Would there be a comedown?

The wind hit me, then Tilda soon came from the toilet and we were gone with no more than a smile in his direction. We trudged about in the mud, linking arms from stage to stage to catch our favourite bands. But I couldn't shift my mind from him.

'If I fall, you fall with me'

Eventually,

We watched The Strokes followed by Kasabian and rushed back to the main stage for Muse before I suggested we return to VIP. Tilda obliged without question. As the sky turned from blue to grey, to a darker shade of blue and then black, the rain only got heavier and poured faster with each change of colour. Slowly and slowly the only shelter in the VIP area, a rather large marquee tent housing a small DJ booth and a bar, became crowded. I spotted him again in the tent then. 80's music exclusively filled our ears, almost drowning out the sounds of rain against the plastic roof. I would glance at him in between conversation with Tilda. He was always watching. I think we were the only ones who could appreciate the irony of dancing in close proximity to damp strangers, whilst singing along to *I Want To Break Free*. That was when he decided to come over.

He wrapped his arm around my back and leaned into my ear.
"I've been watching you all night."

I could feel the heat rushing to my cheeks, but answered with a cool "Yeah, I noticed."

His first glance at Tilda was only when he asked how we came to be here, and I thanked my long-time friend for our tickets. I reciprocated his questions and discovered he was here with work.

"It's our first time playing here, actually. I always came here as a kid with my parents, so it's kind of surreal to be on the other side of the barriers."

I could have guessed he was in a band, with his clean clothes so foreign amongst the mud, but my mind was straying elsewhere. I was conscious that Tilda was listening to our every word so was more than happy to discover that our paths would soon cross in two weeks time at another festival. And with those words, I hung onto an empty promise of *two weeks time.*

Tilda soon dropped her curiosity about him, the rain stopped and we decided it was time to go back to the campsite, at which point she started rambling about her favourite parts of the night. I only had one.

During those early, sodden stages of introductions to his band members, sound men, and managers I was at my most anxious. Anxious with fear that they wouldn't approve. Or worse: they would think I was in it for who or what he was. But the truth is, I didn't even know who he was. I only knew him as the stranger I locked eyes with amid strangers and songs. The stranger whom I simply couldn't get out of my head. First for his looks, and then his charm, touch, scent and words. I think once they saw how happy he was, and how he looked at me, they were happy for him. In fact, I think once they saw how *I* looked at *him* they knew how I felt. I'm sure there were moments where I glimpsed hesitation in an approach towards us, from friends. Maybe for fear of intruding, as if a look given to one another could show so much intimacy. I don't think a word could really tell that stage before love, but that's what we were in; the age of discovery.

—

Back to the car in the November night
I drove 86 miles to find sleep
after speaking to a policeman
he was friendly
I wondered what his life was like
did he have a wife
I stayed up 23 hours to hear you sing
and leaving you seemed bittersweet
as much as it was to close my eyes
and say goodbye to that night

—

Aside from the divine face Bryce pulled when a burst of laughter would escape him, the way his clothes seemed to have been crafted by gods and gifted to him neatly pressed, perfectly fitted and second best only to see him without any at all, it was his way with words that I was so struck by. Not his song lyrics, or the *sound* of his voice, though both were exquisite, the way he always seemed to know what to say. He made me laugh a lot, he made cheeky jokes, he complimented me just the right amount, and his smooth southern accent was just the cherry on top.

I could feel his eyes hovering over me as he introduced me to Willis, the bass player in his band. It was an unusually kind last few weeks of summer, August bank holiday, and the last festival we would both see that year. He was shorter than Bryce, but his eyes were just as friendly and we got on instantly - though I found it hard to concentrate to almost anything he said when Bryce was by my side, churning butterflies and rhapsodies in my stomach with his touch, smoothing up and down my waist, unseen by others. When I had the chance at glancing his way, a smirk was subtly growing, spreading across his face.

Bryce left me in the company of Willis while he spoke with others in a trail towards the bar. Willis suggested we go back to the tour bus to take advantage of free drinks and shade against the sun. He led the way past a high vis coated security guard, and we followed the path we had taken hours before.

Around the back of the main stage, boxes upon boxes of sound equipment were being loaded, much the same as it had when we arrived. It was like the fax machine of an office. The way instruments and amplifiers were methodically rotated on and off stage after each act, often marked with weathered stickers or band artwork.

A large man was struggling with a box that told me The Pigeon Detectives had recently played, and I was momentarily saddened to realise we had missed their set.

We passed the dressing room area, which were really just pop up plastic buildings, square and small in size, which I'd grown accustomed to seeing by now, and where Bryce's tour manager was often busy on her laptop if she weren't busy trying to relocate the band to get onto the bus and leave for the next gig. It wasn't time to leave yet though. The dressing rooms still spilling with people in the six o'clock light, enjoying the company of bands they'd surely seen on the festival route over the summer, with boxes of beer by their side.

Not long after we located the bus did Willis' smile easily lead my finger into a small bag of white substance from his pocket. I don't know why I did it, I didn't feel pressured, nor had I ever done drugs before. But everything in that moment was foreign to me. I wasn't used to that kind of environment, seeing musicians I'd idolised as a child in front of me, hearing them laugh at my friends jokes. I foolishly felt it was right. And after the chemicals left my tastebuds and joined the vodka inside of me, I got a taste for something good. Little did I know just how much that taste would stay with me, after years of forgetting it.

I think my recklessness and impulsiveness went hand in hand, and what might happen afterwards I didn't think about because I knew that Bryce would be by my side: a safety I was already too reliant on. I'd spent my entire life feeling independent. But that summer was the first of my dependency traits. I knew it could only be a bad thing. Dependency traits that were likely encouraged by the girls who fawned for him.

The feeling of tire
when stimulation is paramount
make a decision
do you
take me to feel more
see sunlight through
or withdraw
feel cold
the fright
tension
but you might
sleep

Initially, he downplayed his success. This modesty left me taken aback and weirdly amused with reactions from strangers - *girls*. I could feel their eyes on me when we decided to take a walk to watch Joy Division during one of our first festivals together, the first weekend of July. A sad part of me liked it, knowing that although we had just met, he was mine. More mine than theirs anyway.

As we approached the tent where the band were due to play in ten minutes, girls approached him. It seemed the sticky mud that squelched and glued itself to our shoes was replaced by the eyes of girls as we stepped onto the metal floored barriers in the tent, who would've stuck to Bryce all day if they could have. They knew his name and asked for a picture: I took it for them. They didn't thank me, just left with a questioning look. Bryce seemed amused. He led me by the hand towards the left of the stage where a man stood guard. Those passes on our legs were like keys here. He let us through the barrier and gave us a new pass to stick to ourselves. This time it said 'Joy Division' which sat nicely below the first that read 'The Volants'. The Volants were a new favourite of mine, Bryce being the motive: watching his fingers press along his guitar, and his lips heat a microphone while I watched from the side, was probably only beaten by having him to myself as we watched someone else do the same.

We walked up a set of stairs after passing another man requesting to see our passes, then onto the side of the stage where the band would soon be. There were no others here except someone doing sound checks on the instruments. We stood behind the vast electronic screens that would soon light up to show the crowd live footage of the stage. Slightly translucent, we could see everyone through it. It was odd to be on this side, after all those years spent on the other. They were all looking in our direction, but not at us. Or maybe they were. I wasn't sure if they could see us. Were they wondering who we were? How we got here? *How on earth did I get here?*

So many people stood in front of us yet it felt like we were in a world of our own. Even before, when I was with Tilda in those hot crowds, it had been special. But to be with Bryce here, it felt like only the two of us existed. The rest were insignificant, in the distance, none distracting. And the music that would soon play would merely be an attempt at distraction. It would play, and we might sing along a little, and feel that warm fuzz of excitement at the pure happiness in the nostalgia we all personally wove into the song, but even that would fail to fully distract from the feelings that were slowly but surely intensifying with each minute more spent with one another.

Suddenly the crowd started roaring, the lights went black and four men I recognised as Joy Division walked past us. The drummer smiled at me and clapped hands with Bryce before running onto the stage - they knew each other. I never knew the extremity of his fame, but moments like this made me realise just how much he downplayed his own success.

His arms curled around my waist as he stood behind me swaying to the music whilst they played, a flavour of summer and smoke in the air. Some of the songs I didn't know, but I pretended to while my mind whirled at his touch. After the third, I turned around to face him. He looked at me as if he'd been waiting to see my face again. Unblinking, I held his gaze for a while before slowly edging closer. He met me halfway and kissed me for the first time, then. My body pressed lightly against him; I ran my fingers through his dark curls. He was sweating from the heat of the tent and I tasted it between our kisses, cold on my hands. He was a better flavour than all summers and smoke combined. A better high than anything Willis could offer.

Love Will Tear Us Apart started playing and I squealed in excitement.

"Yay, I know this song!" I broke free from his kiss to dance. He laughed at my elation and watched me spin. The speakers were so close I could feel the music more than I could hear it. I closed my eyes and felt the fuzz around my toes matching the beat of the song. Completely on our own next to thousands of people who were, like me, sweating and dancing to a band they loved. Who were surely weaving their own nostalgia into the songs played, the same as I. And Joy Division's *Love Will Tear Us Apart* soon became the comfiest and most eloquently woven memory made on my playlists, that I could forever listen to, close my eyes and live that first kiss all over again. And I opened my eyes and I loved him. It only took two weeks for me to realise.

Browns Coffee

We agreed to meet for coffee in Crystal Palace. Bryce lived in Victoria but said he didn't mind driving to see me. He said it was his thinking time, his time to sing and churn lyrics into songs I might one day listen to on the radio.

He was earlier than I and had ordered for the both of us. Two steaming drinks sat on the round table. It was still very warm, mid-September and 25 degrees. The thought of a hot drink wasn't the most appealing, but I was glad he'd ordered it once it hit my lips. I tasted liquor and chocolate.

A short man with a greasy ponytail and bright green apron came over to our table to tell us that the shop was closing in ten minutes. Before that, I don't think either of us had realised how close we were to each other. We'd been leant on the table, I don't know how long for, but my elbows were glad for the sudden change in position. He'd spent most of the time asking about my family, my upbringing, and of course, my music taste that by the time we left it felt unfair. He now knew more than most about me, whilst I only knew as much about him as when I arrived; hanging on to what little I had learned about him at those now-distant summer festivals.

"I feel like I've just spoken about myself for the past few hours, I barely know your last name." I reflected as I picked up my bag from the floor.

"Does that mean I'll be seeing you soon?" He held the door open for me, waiting for a reply.

I smiled and walked out into the street, a little cooler now.

"Who says I want to know your last name?" I teased and shivered a little.

"It seemed like you were pretty interested at those festivals the other week."

I shivered again in the cold of the shade, and at the painful reminder that *that* summer was now over. He put his jacket over my shoulders. The sun was setting already, at only 7 pm. But it threw a beautiful glow of orange across the buildings of Crystal Palace. It made me think about how I liked this time of day.

"That's really not necessary, I live around the corner." I accepted his jacket anyway, hugging it into my chest. It smelt of leather, aftershave and tobacco. Bryce was leaning against the wall of the coffee shop, taking out a cigarette and lighter from the back pocket of his jeans.

"Bird," he said, speaking between the cigarette now in his mouth, amused at my confusion. "That's my last name. Bird."

Damn it. I knew I loved this man.

"What're you up to now?"

Was that an invitation? "Probably just reading scripts." I was an actress, but he knew all about me by now.

"I can show you the sights of Victoria?" He took a long drag of his cigarette and let his eyes give me that look of a smile, waiting for an answer.

"You know I've lived in London for three years, right?"

"You know I don't actually care what we do, we can discuss that in the car." And he led the way, knowing I would follow.

I was torn between playing hard to get and succumbing to my weaknesses and lying naked on his kitchen worktop. I had a weird sense of trust in him like I'd known him for years, though it had only been a few short months since that first glance. But maybe women felt the same way about serial killers, and maybe I was on my way to my own death.

Regardless, we sat in his car on Battersea Bridge, heading north in slow-moving traffic: the London Eye tormenting us with its only now seemingly fast pace. He'd given me control of the music and—I have to say—I was doing pretty well.

By the time we reached a side street in Victoria, we'd gone through an entire 80's alternative playlist, reminiscing when *I Want To Break Free* had played. Bryce led the way to his house after casually name dropping some friends he had in the area. I doubted it was his way of impressing me, but more that he was letting his guard down. Comfort was forming between us, and it made me happy to think that he didn't have to hide this side of his life from me.

"I've been here two years now," he said proudly, unlocking the door of a largely bricked, cream house. He led me inside, holding my hand. *Fuck*, my blood was racing. How long had it been since a guy did that? Had a guy ever even done that?

He closed the door.

Hannibal

As I sat reflecting on our first time together, I felt a sense of nostalgia. Though he was right here with me I also felt a new kind of sadness, and he watched as it spread across my face.

"What's wrong?" He sat up and pulled the straps of my vest back onto my shoulders.

"Just thinking about when we met that time in Crystal Palace." Rooted in pain, a short laugh escaped me. What if he left me? What if he toured America and never came back? Maybe he would meet another girl and stay with her, or get into an accident and die.

The pain was only more intense because we were more than compatible with each other, and if I believed in them, I'd say we were soulmates. We were exactly where we were supposed to be, even if that was nights spent on the sofa. But me and my stupid brain couldn't just be content with that. The intrusion of these thoughts frosted the glass doors of my vision. They made me think I'd already lost him, until his touch warmed them away, bringing me back to him again.

"I'm right here," he said, cupping my face with his hands, forcing me to look him in the eyes. *But for how long?* I was mourning the loss of someone still here, who might still be here for years to come, who would maybe have to mourn the loss of me someday. With his face so close to mine, he waited for my phantom grief to pass, for me to return to him.

"I'm ruining Hannibal night aren't I?" I exhaled at my stupidity. A tear escaped the corner of my eye, wiped quick with the outer of his fingers.

"Never."

I guided his hands back onto the straps of my vest. He moved them to fall down the same as before.

"I love you," he whispered, and roughly grabbed me into a bear-like hug, tackling me to the cushions of the sofa. We fell in a clumsy laughter, and when our breaths slowed into silence, I felt him hard against me.

Our next kiss was harder than usual, our teeth colliding as we undressed one another as if our whole relationship was etched into tonight. The day we met, the first time he touched me, the first time I inhaled his breath, his body. When we'd first showered together, cooked together and every night we had spent since.

We rolled onto the stone floor, nothing but the sounds of our bodies sticking and unsticking from one another.

Bryce stood up abruptly, his eyes never leaving mine."I'll be back."

I looked up at the ceiling and placed my hands over my bare breasts, hard from his touch and the cold of the room. He came back in with something behind his back. But my eyes were on his face, they moved down his body taking him in. He was beautiful. I loved him, but right now it was more than that: I needed him. My hands moved from my breasts and caressed my entire body as he watched. And then there he was. His mouth followed where my hands had been, and his words cast heat on my stomach.

"You are so beautiful." His voice hovered around my thighs. He opened a bottle of liquor taken from behind him and poured some onto my stomach, catching it with his tongue as it slid across my body. Then he moved to my lips. I could taste it on him and closed my eyes as I felt the weight of his body against mine. He entered me and all I could do was think of now and how good it all felt. I bit his lip and moaned as we moved together. My lower back scraped against the floor - a pain much welcomed. He pulled my hair hard, the way I liked and we both finished. He carried me to bed a while later. I vaguely recall seeing 3.45 am on the clock by our bed before drifting into a deep sleep, too deep to remember my dreams.

I woke late.

—

Orange shapes
concealed the white
and shocked my eyes
into awakening
his spot was still warm
and sounds were cluttered
the smell of toast
a hum of radio
last night playing
my first thoughts of the morning
followed by breakfast

—

Eventually,

Nature's Playlist

—

Let my door slam
wind windows down
sing that same song

breath

park in the same spot
wind windows up
explore the same plot
of land
it's mine

—

Those autumn days were woven with amber, brown, and gold; the leaves that were one by one being plucked from trees by wind himself until they fell lightly upon the ground, hiding the path ahead. They gave the floor the same colour as above, where trees blocked all sight of the sky and offered your eyes only autumnal colours to look upon. I would walk over the leaves with a crunch in my step, and squint trying to remember the routes from past summers spent there. With so many small opening in the trees, I'd gratefully take a wrong turning or two, which gave me the excuse to climb old stone walls that rose between water and dirt to perform my balancing act — jump, hop and weave around nettles or holly — until I met the path again.

But I never felt lost. Just an overwhelming excitement at the feeling of becoming a child again; sporadic bursts of energy would see me happily cavorting down hills in a zigzag shape, with my arms spread wide like an aeroplane, smiling and humming. Reality would only strike when the occasional walker greeted me with a 'hello'.

I would stroke the trees as I passed them, some damp with moss, others rough with patterns of bark twisting upward, lightly scratching against my touch.

A tree lay fallen, bathing its branches in the reservoir below, inviting ducks to perch and congregate with one another, unaffected by my passing. I wondered, more hoped, whether they would have begun to recognise me. I often threw seeds into the lake and watched them dive to catch them, before they sank to the floor and became lost in the stone and earth. I hoped they would grow to like me and expect food with each visit.

I would always run across the field after parking my car at the brow. But, upon reaching the forest, I would take my time amongst the trees: for they shielded me from the cold. They left the breeze to play nicely above the branches, waiting until I was once more exposed, stealing back the warmth the trees had so kindly given me.

Oh, the trees.

There were three reservoirs. At the top of the third, I could see everything: my car parked in the distance, the trailing path which seemed so much clearer from above. Here was always the perfect place to catch breath, watch the vigorous winds shake the trees in the distance, and truce with whatever battle I'd commenced in my head that day.

The sun would fall differently each day, at different times, with different shades and shapes of cloud - though sometimes there were none. More often than not, on a clear night before the light left, a thin haze of purple would cast itself along the bottom of the sky, visible over the waters of the reservoir, so bright and deep in colour it distracted me from everything else. You could look at it until it disappeared.

And just like each day when the sun moved differently, so would I. And I never grew bored. Because each week the colours would change, crisp leaves would fall and then be trodden into the dirt, soggy. More trees would occasionally fall, often rain too, so although the place remained, it was different every time.

Where the rivers would run high in winter, nothing but rocks would be visible in spring, then blackberries blossomed in summer. I sought them in Autumn, but found only their shrivelled remains in the September cold. And although I didn't have any blackberries, the autumn brought with it that familiar squelch of mud beneath my feet, not dissimilar to that of English festivals. A comforting feeling, no less.

There was one particularly quiet patch that I usually found towards the end of my walks. From under a wooden bridge, water dived into a small lake and gave birth to bubbles of air that soon popped as they moved with the current. The water looked so clear it made me thirsty.

I often jumped over the small bridge and paddled barefoot in the water, running my feet under the weight of the current. The disturbance of my foot would quickly unearth the dirt beneath the rocks and turn the clear water murky, momentarily, but would soon return clear almost as quickly as my feet turned numb.

I never wanted to grow up, but remain the child we adults fought so hard to conceal. We spend our younger years trying to mimic our parents, while all they crave is our youth. We feel controlled by our parents, yet have all the freedom in the world to do what adults should not: express our freedom. Express however the hell we want. We can cry, we can skip, we can make funny faces and speak freely in public without fear of judgement. The adults are controlled by money, sex, power and above all, their reputation. They are trapped in their own little persons, but they have locked themselves in.

Oh, how special it would be if adults would forget their worries at the sight of adventure, and mystery, and games. If only adults would swing on the swings, roll in the mud, get caught in the rain without a phone in their pocket to worry about, maybe their lives would be filled with a little more joy like those of children. If only they joined me instead of pulling looks of disapproval, maybe they too could feel what I feel when I am amongst the trees.

And all too soon the night would creep along unexpectedly, and I would get lost and maybe panic beneath the darkness of the trees, to then find light again on the field before my car and laugh at the fear that moments ago consumed me: reminding me of how fragile those thoughts could be. How quickly one could escape fear or loneliness or angst if only they realised their own potential to do so. To *change*.

With the occasional tap of the dashboard and hum to a song, I'd be home.

My days were birch, pine, and oak. My nights lavender, that easily led me to sleep, allowing the aches to ooze from my body before waking at next light with a need to create more. More aches that came with so much freedom in those afternoons at the reservoirs.

—

Watch me as my skin turns
a shade of blue it burns
the rain is unkind to me today
oh god my skin hurts
but I tell you it was well worth
the cold that so dearly clings to me

—

Green Peppers

I was half awake. My eyes still toying with sleep. It was my mouth that led my body into awakening. The smell of food drifted up and back out of my nose, diluting the dryness caused by sleep. Sleep that my body had finally succumbed to.

Breakfast was beans, two veggie sausages, browned on both sides, with a shiny glaze of oil dripping from each, seeping into my tomatoes. The tomatoes were halved and blackened on the top, wrinkled skin still intact around the edges. And green peppers. I hated green peppers. Why had he given me green peppers?

I reached for the ketchup after giving them a moody scrape across to the edge of my plate. Too much slid from the bottle. Was it going to be one of those days?

I reached for the bread and margarine sitting in the middle of the table. The margarine was too cold and when planted onto my slice, it scraped a hole through the middle. *Yes, One of those days.*

Bryce came from behind with a pot of tea and kissed the side of my eye as he passed me and sat opposite.

"Good morning."

I smiled.

"I'm in the studio today."

...

"Only for a few hours, should be back before dinner."

I interrupted his bite of toast with a kiss across the table. An

AC/DC shirt of his that I'd thrown on this morning dipped itself into my breakfast. I rolled my eyes and threw it off, sitting naked - eating breakfast.

"Thank you, Bryce."

"It feels strange when you say my name, you never say my name." His eyes rolled over my body but he said nothing.

"I should say it more often. Bryce. Bryce. *Bryce.*" The last one merely a whisper.

I picked at my breakfast, around the green peppers. He was clearly relieved by my cheeriness this morning.

"You make a good breakfast."

"I know."

"Except I hate green peppers." I looked up from my knife and fork, reading his expression. It looked as if he was suppressing a laugh.

"I know." He looked at his plate. No green peppers. I laughed.

"I'm eating your breakfast aren't I?"

"I'm sad you think so little of me."

We ate in a serene silence before he rushed to leave when Willis beeped from his car outside. He kissed me goodbye and left me with nothing but green peppers on my plate.

The Garden

I decided to wash the remains of last night from my skin. It took two rounds of shower gel to feel clean. The hairs of my freckled arms raised as I stepped from the shower and onto the mat - I had forgotten a towel. I stood for a minute with my feet nestling into the soft cotton that cocooned around my toes, and welcomed the shelter from the breeze gliding around my body. It absorbed the drips that tickled my skin and turned the emerald mat to a darker shade of green, almost black.

A new day. I liked being alone sometimes. As much as I loved him, I needed space. Space to think and observe and appreciate other things: a reminder that there was more to life than him. To remember what bought me joy before I found him. I often took long walks around those reservoirs by our house, empty in the weekdays, but flocked with walkers and families at weekends.

Space from him meant I didn't cloud over everything else in my life. My mind had space to wander. But sometimes the feet of my mind strayed, like I often did around those reservoirs, to the darker paths of my mind. The ones he so easily guided me away from when here, but left my walking boots and took the map every time he left.

I decided to cloud my lungs instead. I threw on a clean shirt from his drawer and felt the cold wood of the porch steps against my bare skin. I was completely exposed to the lazy, moping breeze tickling my ankles, but at ease knowing our house was secluded for miles around, rolling hills standing before us. I left my legs to fall where they pleased and re-lit the cigarette blown out by the wind. I cupped my hand and curled my lips around the filter waiting to see red again. Bliss.

I took a deep drag and closed my eyes. I waited a few seconds, holding the smoke in my lungs before exhaling. I enjoyed it now. What used to be weak wisps of smoke hovering in my mouth, trying to impress a man I barely knew, were now breaths so dense it took two exhales for my breath to clear. It scared me because I knew I'd changed. As if something so damaging didn't bother me anymore. As if the fear that once consumed me when the smell hit my nose had evaporated. How could something so easily replace breakfast when he wasn't here to cook it?

Change was inevitable but it made it no less welcoming. Something I was always so sure about had changed in a heartbeat because of one single man. It made me question everything in my life and I wondered what would change next. What other things that now stood adamant inside me would soon collapse?

I watched the sun cast shadows in front of me, unveiled by indistinguishable sad clouds in dull shades of grey. It told me to get up and start my day. But I liked these days. They reminded me of my childhood spent walking with my parents and sister, ears popping, sweating beneath waterproofs while our ears and hands froze from the air that gripped to them. Mother would carry the flasks in her obscenely small rucksack, while Rose and I would fashion sticks that would serve as wands, walking apparatus, swords or pencils to mark the dirt with doodles. The air was always cold, just like today. You could almost taste it against your throat like cold water, making the warmth from the flasks even more welcoming. Except, instead of quenching our thirst with hot chocolates and jam biscuits at the top of hills, in caves, or perched on stone bridges now too narrow for today's means of transport, I now sat hydrating my thirst for nicotine. *Bliss.*

The Decision

I found three missed calls from my agent waiting on my phone when I went back inside. Alongside that, a script in my inbox. It sat printed and stapled on the passenger seat of my Jeep ten minutes later. I drove away from home, somewhere unfamiliar, to become someone else. As an actress, I could transform myself and leave my own thoughts behind. I could discover a character's motives, their mannerisms, weaknesses and passions. I would forget myself like I did when I was with Bryce. I thrived off of my work. Because the truth was—since being with him—being alone had became progressively more difficult.

When I wasn't with Bryce or working, I'd think about life, death, and all of the things that scared me: failure, disappointing the ones I loved, where I might end up in ten years time. I would think and think until my thoughts were interrupted by his arrival, or until I had a panic attack and fell into nightmare-ridden sleep in patches of my own sweat. So finding a script in my inbox was much welcomed on a day like today when Bryce would be out until dark. Today I would meet somebody new in those papers that sat next to me. Who would they love? Who would *I* soon love? I had affairs with every role.

I pulled into a small village after driving along the narrow, winding roads. It was a place I'd never visited, despite it being only an hour or so from the church. The air felt colder and the wind stronger than this morning. I should've brought a jacket. I stood at the edge of the village by a small set of public toilets and a visitors centre. In the distance, I could see an old town hall no bigger than a church. Between myself and the hall stood old terrace buildings made from hand carved stone, how old I couldn't say. Some were houses, one a bicycle shop, another a fresh grocery stall with produce sat cooly outside its doors, and at the end of the street - a tea room.

It looked a little busy but empty tables were visible. I ordered a black coffee and sat in the corner I thought to be furthest from any noise.

Tomorrow I would be driving to London for the audition, so I got started right away, excited to embody whatever was in those pages in front of me. But my eyes soon hovered over the same sentence multiple times, too distracted by a conversation that my ears couldn't ignore.

"When were you intending on retiring?"

A business meeting I assumed. I glanced up. My eyes glancing upon each table until I recognised the same voice from a greying man in a navy suit, his stomach bulging from his white shirt, large brown shoes tapping along to the quiet hum of the cafe. Sat opposite him was a young, rather large woman wearing a hoodie and blue jeans. She looked uncomfortable, stretching the sleeves of her jumper over her fists as the man spoke. He began a rather dull speech about pensions and death.

"It's just unfortunate for the loved ones really." He stretched back into his chair, patting his stomach. "All the bills you don't think about, any debts you have? It goes straight to the ones closest to you, you see."

Silence

"Now, with your income, I don't expect you'll want to leave any charitable donations?"

Slightly patronising, he reminded me of a school teacher. But a little more insensitive.

He leaned forward. "What kind of cancer do you have?"

I thought he should've maybe invested in a private office for this kind of *business* meeting. Anger built inside me at the endurance this woman had to maintain.

"Cervical…only stage one though." She flashed a polite smile which quickly vanished.

"As a man, I squirmed a bit then." He chuckled and gestured to his lower stomach.

I cringed. I couldn't concentrate here, his lacking tasteful manner leaving the depths of my coffee with little appease, so I left it there, half full, and decided to take a walk.

Walking back towards my car, away from the village, I meandered my way through a kissing gate that marked the start of a snaking path to fields and hills beyond. I followed it, with only my script and notebook in hand, up the hill made by walkers who'd treaded their heels in the same spots so much the grass no longer grew. I was out of breath when I came to a cluster of rocks upon the top of the ascent, a steep drop beyond. I sat and took in the view, not caring for the damp that might mark my bottom. It was quiet here. Finally, a place to read in peace.

Soon my stomach became too noisy to ignore and the pages of my notebook had been turned, inked, and creased by the wind.

The socks around my ankles became wet on the descent to my car. And clouds seemed to only thicken as the day went on, giving speckles of rain to the ground infrequently.

I realised my body was numb with cold once I slammed the Jeep shut and powered the engine, blasting the heat to life with a harsh jerk of the nob to the right. It stung my skin where the cold had been sat for so long so I decided to open the windows slightly to ease the intensity. It reminded me of when I was younger.

Every Sunday I had played football for the local girls' team and nearly every match I would leave with numb toes and icy arms. I often bathed as soon as I got home, so fast that the rash from the cold weather would soon turn to hot aches from the burn of the water against my thighs and feet. It would hurt so much that I'd hover them under the flow of the cold tap until feeling regained.

I showered now. Unbuckling and escaping the trap of my jeans, I stepped under the hard hits of heat from the shower head and felt a release. As if I had been holding my breath the entire ride home, tense with cold. It felt good. I let water trickle into my mouth and spat it out methodically. As the water filled my mouth, my mind filled itself with those thoughts I'd spent all morning ignoring. I turned the shower colder as my body temperature suddenly rose with panic. My heart worked hard and fast. I thought I could hear it pounding through my ears, but could *feel* it in my chest at a different rate as if I had two.

I saw speckles of red dots appear and disappear around the corners of my vision and sank my naked body to slump amongst shampoo bottles and stray body hairs, exhaling my breath into the rolls of my stomach. I tried to focus, tried to calm myself like usual. My hands moved over my breasts, listening to my heartbeat. I screwed my face up as hard as I could and then released it. I spoke the alphabet backwards to take my mind elsewhere. I counted to ten in Spanish, spoke about the weather in French. Anything. Then soon enough, my heart slowed and the cold returned. Remaining seated, I shoved the shower dial off and sat feeling the last drops of water escaping onto my head.

drip, drip, drip.

Work easily led my mind, like a dog on a lead, from the darker places it so often delved to. But my work was the walker, my troubled thoughts the dog; likely a Doberman, a Great Dane, a dog too strong for its owner.

I had trouble with my intrusive thoughts. They started with a fearful idea and progressed into a novel of negativity about the fictional paths that might one day turn into an autobiography. And once those fingers of my mind got typing, my own world didn't even exist anymore. I couldn't actively think, so submerged inside those pages. I was just a shell, filled with darkness and things that weren't even real.

I thought about death a lot. *How I would die? Would it be self-inflicted?* And I had trouble with my past. I thought a lot about mistakes I'd made over the years and how I could right them, how I'd live my life differently, should I have the chance. Then I wondered whether I *would* right them. Maybe I didn't need to right them, maybe they were necessary for my growth.

What kept me sane was the idea that everything happened for a reason. That each little thing in life would lead you to where you are now. That maybe I needed to make those mistakes. Maybe they had led me to Bryce. And if I hadn't have made those mistakes, I would have met someone else - and that was what I couldn't quite fathom. Not my excessive interpretations of quantum mechanics and the endless possibilities of multiple universes in existence, but that in one of those different lives, different universes, I could actually love somebody equally, or even more so, than Bryce.

If I'd have gotten up earlier today, maybe I'd have spilt boiling coffee on myself or tripped and hit my head on the wrong side of the curb and died before I reached my car - *one universe gone.* If I'd have chosen to walk to school growing up maybe I'd have gotten to the playground at a different time and become friends with a completely different group of girls who would've shaped me into a completely different person, taught me that my favourite colour is, in fact, sky blue, not emerald. They might have encouraged me to drink more at parties and walk home intoxicated, I wouldn't have noticed the man following me - *another universe gone.*

If I'd have gotten that cameo in the feature film I auditioned for last summer I would've never met Bryce.

I like to think that failure always proceeds with success. Or to put into better words: success is often a result of a failure, of lessons learned or motivations born from the feeling of failure; a want for it not to happen again. Failure can impel your motive. But my mind liked to remind me more of the failures than the successes in my life. And so I was often thrown into my work as an actress to distract from these wild theories and thoughts that kept me up at night and made me sweat even in the coldest of showers.

Maybe that's why I got a call two days later telling me I'd got the part. I cried, of course. This was a big deal. *A lead role.* The first of many to come Bryce said to me when I broke the news to him. I cried again.

"Do you know what this means though?" I was hesitant.

"I don't care what this means, this is no different from me going on tour. Where is it shooting?" He was nothing but smiles.

"Utah…after Christmas."

We held each other's gaze as if it were our last. It was late November. At least we'd have Christmas together.

"Three months."

He hugged me and said nothing more than 'congratulations'. I knew he meant it. And I knew that I would take it, and my decision was made and I was going to Utah to star in my first film.

—

And maybe this
was the beginning of the end
the end of our love
I'd spent so long cherishing
the end of a book
I longed to never finish
but longed to know it's ending

and a new book is found
before the last is finished
upon a heap I never thought I'd search
with a plot so juicy and wet
an evasion to the last
so hard to put down
making the first
only a memory
making me question
which will I finish first

—

Change

I was here. The air was cold, snow falling but failing to remain on the ground. 4 pm greeted me with Christmas trees at the entrance of the hotel. I always hated that. Why did we not just take them down on Boxing Day? I didn't want to think about the joys of Christmas, or of how long it would be until the next.

***

The lead up to Christmas had been filled with a counterfeit smell of oncoming snow so we had heavily stocked the pantry with oats, rice, tins of beans, mushy peas, and sweetcorn. Vegetables were now growing in abundance in the greenhouse: onions, chard, asparagus and carrots. So Bryce and I had spent an entire week without leaving the surroundings of the church, with plenty of food to fill our bodies and land around us to tire our legs.

We spent almost an entire afternoon weighing down branches of the tree with decorations while listening to Christmas singles on Bryce's record player. With the exception of a few fairy lights looped around the wooden beams of the ceiling, the tree was our only festive piece. We needed no more.

No bauble was the same. A few resembled snow globes, glass and fragile, with a delicate dusting of snow coating the floor of the world inside. Others included a fabric stitched gingerbread man made by my younger self, a 3D glittered David Bowie face which hung with a thread the same colour as his plastic hair, a ceramic cassette player, a sushi roll, and one leather, mimicking a baseball collected by Bryce during a writing trip to Chicago.

Ostensibly, they all matched. Each collected at different times, each different in size, shape, colour and texture. But together they made for the most complimented tree. And we sat right by it, our legs reddening by the fire, as we opened the few gifts between us and cards from distant relatives on Christmas Day. It had all been perfect. A quiet affair, but perfect. As much as any other day spent with Bryce.

***

I removed my wet shoes at the door of my room, 505, and fell face first onto my bed. My suitcase was heavy and after 20 hours of travelling, I was glad I could finally empty it into the room I would call home for the next month. After this first month in Salt Lake, we were heading to Vegas, then spending the final month in Varese, Italy.

Tomorrow was my first day on set. I was excited to start, to meet my co-stars and the crew. To get my own trailer and read my favourite books in between takes.

The crew had already started shooting scenes a few weeks prior to my arrival. I'd seen two news articles about the film and I was excited. They flew me first class - a first. This trip was going to be full of firsts, I could tell.

***

I spent my time in the airport's private lounge innocently amused with a plush chair that spun me around. I was alone except for a man in a suit with a thick greying moustache, filling a paper plate at the snack bar with blueberry cupcakes and ham sandwich triangles. He glanced over at me, smiled, then proceeded to the furthest table from me to eat his selection of carbs in peace.

The effect of the spinning chair was not enough to see me through the entire three-hour wait, so when the time came I was more than ready for my second flight from Orlando to Salt Lake City.

In between, I sat spinning slowly, reading news articles about the film. My name hadn't appeared yet despite being the lead.

'Grace Winter teases first looks on the set of Away Game'.

There was a picture of Grace on set with her phone in hand, talking to the director, taken by paparazzi from a distance. She was pretty.

'Winter will appear alongside an A-list cast in Del Ponzo's latest film, with other leads yet to be announced'.

They didn't know me yet. Part of me scanned each article for my name, hungry for the start of fame. Was I ready for all of this? Was I ready to be more well known than my boyfriend? He who left a trail of teenagers following with excited whispers almost everywhere we went.

I'd experienced it second hand and dealt with the perks of Bryce's fame: the lack of financial worry, the security, the invitations to parties. But I'd dealt with the shit too: the sleepless nights for fear of someone breaking into our home, the paranoia of people following us. The stress of fame was real. But it wasn't *my* fame. So did I really know what I was about to get myself into?

It's not necessarily what I strived for in my career. But being famous meant being successful, and it was that part of me scanning the news articles for my name - a conscious effort for self-validation. To live up to my boyfriend's success, for him to be equally proud. Like I was of him.

Though I enjoyed the walk to Gate 403 in the knowledge that nobody knew me and my greasy hair wouldn't be published on *Variety* the next morning. I boarded my final flight to Salt Lake.

***

I woke in the middle of the night, surrounded by damp sheets and the smell of sweat. I washed my face in the dark of the bathroom and checked my phone for messages. The time was 3.50 am. I had a car picking me up in two hours and ten minutes and decided I wouldn't sleep much until then, so I slid my balcony door open and felt a sharp, cold breeze blow around my feet and move the curtains as it quickly stole the warmth from my room. The automatic light came on. I grabbed a blanket folded neatly at the bottom of my bed and set it on top of the metal of a chair outside. Momentarily the cold felt nice. It woke me from my worries and calmed me, though it didn't last.

I grabbed another blanket and lit a cigarette with a lighter I had stolen from Bryce. I thought of him. What time was it at home?

It took two rings for him to answer.

"Kora," he sighed down the phone, happy to hear my voice. I smiled in response. Wow, this was hard already.

"I can't sleep."

"Are you ready?" He was worried.

"For what?" I couldn't hide the tension in my voice. I swallowed tears.

"I don't know…, everything."

"The film, yes. I can't wait." I couldn't keep the strain from my voice.

"You got this." I could hear his pride.

"It's going to be a long three months."

"It's going to be the best three months of your life, I promise."

Scene 3, Exteriors

—

Birds sat on the T
in a neat little row of three
down the aisle
they lit the way
for the night drivers
the ones wired
with caffeine
or substance
inebriating their conscious away
from those defined by blue and red
suburbs of the forest
winding like rivers
overgrown in parts
threatening our tarmacked world
with a sweet taste for what could be without us
we migrate

—

The phone by my bed rang a foreign sound, waking me into a state of confusion, then realisation, then dread.

"Hello?" My voice was croaky.

"Hi miss, you have a car waiting for you outside reception." The woman's smooth American accent would be the first of many I'd hear today.

Shit, shit, shit.

I grabbed clothes from my suitcase and brushed my teeth whilst putting my socks on, toothpaste spraying the air as it clattered against my teeth. Taking the room key from the door, I rushed to the elevator and was in the car only a few minutes later. A great start to the day: too tired to be nervous, too annoyed at myself to focus on my lines.

I wasn't nervous about shooting scenes, but of new introductions; making a good impression was important to me. I needed people to know I was talented, that they had made the right decision in casting me. Though this movie had consumed so much of my life over the two months leading up to now, so much so that that I'd played a game of polygamy between my world with Bryce and that of the character, I really had convinced myself I was the only one for the role. With that thought, a smile lifted my cheeks as I was led to the hair and makeup trailer.

I was told a runner would collect me in two hours time and show me to set. There were too many people to remember names, in and out of the trailer, talking into radios, checking how far along we were from being ready - the usual.

An hour into the curling of my hair, Grace Winter was guided into the chair next to me where the makeup artist started prepping her skin: cleansing, wiping, moisturising. She spoke a general 'hello' to the room but quickly buried her head in a book until we were both led to set. It left me feeling a little disappointed. Unsure why I tried to ignore it and enjoyed the touch of the hair stylist's fingers twining around my scalp instead.

"Kora, right?" She knew my name.

"Yes. It's lovely to meet you." I beamed and foolishly held out my hand as we walked over cardboard and hay that had been laid to form a dry path from the trailers towards the buildings in front of us. She rejected it and hugged me casually from the side. Her eyes were round, big, a beautiful chestnut colour; the first thing I really noticed about her.

"And you," she said, before dropping her gaze.

"So how's it all going? When did you start shooting?" I knew this already from the articles I had read on the way here.

"I came last week but Sasha said they'd all been shooting some landscape stuff a couple' days before. We should run through some lines if you fancy it later. Unless you prefer to just go straight for it on set?"

I agreed, eager to spend more time with a woman I'd spent so long idolising.

Sasha was the director. *Sasha Del Ponzo.* I hadn't met him yet. He hadn't even been at my audition but we had video called to talk about the film and hear me read lines. He seemed cool with his jet black ringlets sitting perfectly around his sharp cheekbones, or his nose ring and the plethora of jewellery worn on his hands, visually loud against his all-black attire.

Though his style was intimidatingly perfect, it was his personality that made me look at him in awe, which made me so keen to hear his thoughts. And the way he spoke to you, the way he *listened* and then the way he didn't listen at all when he became so lost in thoughts that you could see the cogs turning through his steel-cut gaze.

He found all humans fascinating. He watched them, he wrote about them, he made spectacles of them in his films that were serio-comic in style and streamlined in such a way that emotions stung like a razor burn against your throat.

The depths to his thoughts on humans was something special. I was glad he had used that quality and turned it into his career. I had a feeling—or at least hoped—we would be friends for a long time.

In what seemed like a deep conversation, he saw me from over the shoulder of a guy with rolls of tape attached to his trousers and forgot what he was saying.

"Koraaaa!" His gangly arms were thrown into the air before wrapping themselves around me for a hug.

We spoke of the scenes being shot today: close-ups and wide shots of my scene in my house, getting ready for my date to arrive. Grace had a few running in the rain, where the water was already being prepared, and some dialogue between the two of us if we had time.

My 'house' was, in fact, a set built entirely in the studio, only half in existence. As if it had been sawed down the middle perfectly. Where the other half of my house should have been, saw cameramen setting up their dolly tracks and different cameras. It was where everyone rushed and squeezed themselves around others, busy in their own job, while I sat in my makeshift house, getting makeup and hair touch-ups, or running lines with the script supervisor. Except for the set design crew, nobody else was allowed in my half-house. The carpet needed to stay clean.

Lost in the chaos were my phone and coffee amongst the director's chair and viewing screens because multiple people strived for organisation by simply hiding items from sight. After I found my belongings and tranquillity, I headed to catering for food and silence, which was soon welcomely disturbed by Grace.

We were shooting in the city and had only a small hall where caterers served their creations on paper plates. We headed for a quieter spot, which turned out to be behind the building where stacks upon stacks of school chairs were balanced.

Instead of taking one from the pile, Grace jumped and landed sitting on a stack of five chairs, fork in mouth. She picked up her plate and started to pick at falafel and lettuce before looking at me as if to ask if I were joining her.

A little less gracefully, I jumped up to eat my food alongside her. We sat for a while, listening to songs played by the feet of crew members who scurried past. They skimmed like stones on water, before sinking into shallow puddles invisible until trodden on. They fought paper against the wind on their clipboards so much so, we went almost unnoticed our whole time sitting there. With the exception of a few extras who had sought after Grace for a picture or simply the chance to introduce themselves, we were alone. She made me nervous too, but for different reasons. I would catch myself looking too long at her smooth, chocolate skin exposed above her collar or would forget my train of thought when I would start to count every freckle that sat upon her nose.

This became our usual lunch spot, where my lunch break became more cherished than my actual work. But my nervousness didn't fade as the days went by, only heightening as we spoke more. As if it were betokened by a shadow of Bryce: looming, watching, listening. And I became increasingly aware of what I would soon have to tell her.

We were sat once more on the chairs, asking one another impromptu questions about our characters in the film. We often saw the silence after lunch as a chance to practice improvisation.

"Why do you feel sad?" Grace asked.

"Because I miss my family. I don't know, the shit I'm going through. It's when you need your mum the most, isn't it? I've had no letters, nothing."

"And have you sent them many?"

"… Oh, letters? Well, no-"

"Why?"

"I don't know, I just expected them to send something first, you know? Shouldn't she be worried about me?"

"So maybe it's a little of your fault too. Maybe the guilt should be mutual?"

I paused. That word, it clung to me.

"Well?"

Oh shit, "I have been feeling guilty quite a lot recently."

"You only have to let her know how you feel. That usually works."

"You have no idea." I laughed. Grace waited for me to elaborate, not yet aware that the thoughts of my character had long left me.

"I'm in a relationship." *And you're about to mess with it.*

"Oh." There was a quizzing manner to her frown. My character was not at all in a relationship. I laughed and saw her eyebrows jerk with confusion.

"No, you don't understand." The last creases of laughter smoothed as my next sentence formed inside my head.

"You see, I have a boyfriend. But…I'm falling for someone else."

Where before we'd sat with our backs to the chairs, she looked at me now with her body too.

"For who?"

"You." My eyes darted between hers, searching for a response. It felt like a lifetime. She answered me with a touch, gently placing her hands on mine, she squeezed. It was enough. Enough to make me glad I had told her.

The Move In

It was all so scary. Neither of us had owned a house before, we didn't know how the bills worked or why the hot water tap ran cold.

Richard, a man who I'd only ever spoken to on the phone, was holding our keys at his office in the nearest town to our property, ten miles down the road. We both drove our own cars, so dangerously full that neither of us could see through the back windows. I arrived first, while Bryce had gone to collect the keys. I parked up outside the church enclosed with huge draping trees. Should they have been absent, you'd have seen the church from the fields below quite easily.

I stood in silence with the car door still open, looking at what was now our home. It was going to take a lot of work, but even now amongst the piles of mismatch bricks, chunks of wood slowly rotting, and overgrown bushes hiding the porch, I could see it in all of its beauty. It still shone through the years of neglect, wearing it well like ripening fruit.

We spent the next week staying in a bed and breakfast only a few miles away, getting up at 5 am to work through the entirety of daylight, clearing the rubble, garden equipment, and disused church furniture that had been left outside. Skips came and went, struggling along the winding roads until the front doors were clear and we could get to work on the inside. But it was no easier. Cobwebs spun so high we couldn't reach them from the tops of ladders. Bryce soon resorted to bravely jumping, with a duster in hand from atop the ladder, where he finally captured them. Though it seemed his courage was wasted when a new family of spiders greeted us the next day.

We did, however, find a few gems inside amongst the sheer mess of the church's outdated and disused facilities. My favourite was the grand piano which we eventually refurbished.

And soon enough, the space was liveable; we could sleep on an airbed without inhaling any dust.

The move in had been my favourite week. We had spent every minute indoors, diluting the boxes each day. Our dining table a rug on the floor, our television the piano which he often played while I listened by his feet. Our meals were pre-made sandwiches and takeaways because we had no electricity. Bryce spent the remaining days of renovation fixing or replacing parts of the church too old or damaged to repair. I spent them as his assistant or I would read books outside to escape the dust that returned alongside the shrill sound of a drill.

Then came the fun part: Bryce playfully pushing me in a trolley back to the car from the DIY store, foreign laughter escaping my timbre from the rough gravel of the car park. Then, flicking paint from our brushes in between strokes of grey, and finding dots of it on our skin days after. Dots that surely should have washed away long before in the showers that had finally turned warm.

Soon enough we found ourselves boxing up the temporary furniture to give to charity: the airbed, the cheap mugs we had chipped or covered in paint, and an ugly vase that Bryce's grandmother had given us which I'm sure she had, herself, bought from a charity shop. That felt like a weight lifted. Because it told us that we have achieved it all, we finally had a home with matching cups and a *real* bed. And unbeknown to Bryce, no ugly lime vase. We found furniture at local Sunday markets and antique stores, we framed our pictures and piece by piece saw our home come to life.

There were three bedrooms upstairs. Downstairs was an open plan hall much the same as it had been when constructed in the 1800s. We kept a few of the carved stone statues indoors and transferred the others into the garden, too beautiful to give to the skips. We added a large kitchen which, though incredibly modern, fit perfectly with the arched windows and a red velvet bench salvaged from the pews that used to fill the room, but now sat singly by the entrance. I think out of everything, the entrance was my favourite of all. We had not one, but two front doors, wooden, which joined in the same arched shape as the windows. Each with small stain-glass windows in the middle, the doors that were sheltered from the weather on the outside by the entrance hall. It was the only thing that remained from the original building of the church, dating back to the 12th Century.

Upon exchange of the keys, Richard gave us records of the place. We spent our nights engrossed in the fading papers until we became tour guides of our own home. They stated that two architects from London had travelled north to complete a full restoration of the church back in the 1800s, and had done extensive work restoring the tracery in the East and West windows, relaying the floor with stone, and retiling the roof so that very little of the original building was really left. Except for that arched hall which even made stone from the 1800s look new.

In the first week of completion, there was a night I couldn't sleep. I grabbed a few blankets free of Bryce's weight, wrapped them around my naked body and shuffled my way into another room while he slept. The laptop screen startled my eyes but I prised them open onto an empty page and sat with my back against the side of the piano. Reflecting like the light from my screen, I wrote words until my eyes ached and the sky outside was no longer black, but washed with deep waves of purple. I guessed it was around 4 am.

His body radiated the perfect heat
like he was made for me
like a magnet I gravitated
a hand to a glove
he warmed me when cold
filled me when drained
no amount of time
would I grow bored
or the fear of losing him ebb
or reside away like wave from shore
for we were lake and stone
we were stagnant
inert
where we wanted to be
we'd stay a thousand years
and find our bodies a fossil in time
inseparable and intertwined
for I was made for him
and he for I

I rejoined him in bed and gently placed a leg over his body. I was wet against his thigh and he stirred in response. With eyes still closed, his arm disappeared under the sheets and met my body, his fingers sliding inside of me. I moaned. We made love in the dark with nothing but the sounds of our breath and the friction of sheets until we both finished. Laid on our backs, too tired to reach for the blankets that had been lost to the dark around the sides of the bed, we slept for a few more hours and woke to the sound of birds and wind against the stained glass windows.

Some nights were like that: midnight writing and fucking. However they ended, and however they started, they were perfect.

***

I reflected on these memories as I deliberated how I'd tell him I was leaving him.

Eventually,

Progression

I was drunk. I excused myself from her and looked instead at the back of a cubicle door. It felt good sitting there before my inquisitiveness got the better of me and questioned how many others had sat here before me. I hadn't realised how long we'd been standing until now. My feet hurt and my head spun as I closed my eyes and waited for the rest of it to escape me. When drops no longer dripped, my thong twisted as I clumsily slid it back up my legs, onto my hips. I'd peed on my hand. *Lovely.*

Cheap soap was excessively squirted from the dispenser and onto my hand before I flung the tap up. The water sprayed onto my skirt as I washed bubbles away and stung my wrists with the water's heat. Oddly, it felt good, warming me. I was the kind of girl who filled her baths high with water that burned, and tested my body with how much heat it could endure during my daily clean.

I swayed my hands under the dryer, becoming increasingly frustrated by its stupid sensors for not realising I needed to dry my hands. When it finally came to life the sound shocked and then annoyed me. I was glad to leave and get back to her.

She saw me from across the room and gave a smile, lightly mocking my clumsy stumble back to the bar. I only hoped she was as drunk as I. Because I knew what I wanted, what had been playing on my mind, but what was stuck in traffic somewhere in between there and my mouth. I was ashamed of how many drinks it took for me to unclog the traffic jam.

"You're back." She smiled. Her eyes burned me, made me feel vulnerable.

"I'm back." I picked up my mojito and sipped through the straw, pretending to be interested in the mint leaves falling to the bottom of the glass with each sip.

"So."

"Soo..." I laughed nervously, it turned into a quiet fit of giggles, my head heavy.

She began to laugh too. Then she simply sat with a smile, watching me, playing with paper drinks mats on the bar. Her eyes flickered behind me and tensed her back.

"Shall we go back to the hotel?" Her eyes reflected her troubled tone. I stopped laughing, suddenly aware of what might happen at the hotel.

"That's not what I mean." She could read me like a book. "Let's just go back, it's getting late."

"But we're not on set tomorrow. The music's good here!" I felt like a child with her mother on a school night.

Part of me wanted to stay, delay what I wanted, and yet was so wanting of.

"We can stay for one more if you want, I'm just not enjoying this place so much anymore." She must have sensed her own tone, and added: "Besides, they haven't played Bowie in about half an hour."

Her smile couldn't hide the concern etched into her eyes and the lines between her brows. I followed the looks she'd been casting behind me and saw a group of men looking our way, smiling. Not in a friendly way. One wore a black vest showing faded green tattoos down one arm. He looked me in the eye, winked, and I agreed to leave.

There was a queue of taxis lined outside the bar, we took the first and climbed through the sliding doors. She gave the guy our hotel address while I closed my eyes. I'd drank too much. It wasn't a good match for the driver's harsh use of the brakes and acceleration. *Why did they always do that?*

She paid the taxi man and led me to the elevator, greeting the receptionist on our way past. Slotting the key to room 505, I watched her delicate hands open my door, paving the foundation for my fall to the bed, not dissimilar to my first night arriving -

just a tad more drunk. I sat with my face against the covers, neatly arranged by maids, before turning my body with great effort onto my back.

"I *love* Salt Lake City." I enthused.

I heard her laugh from a distance and sat up to look at her. She was stood against the door, concern moulding her brows. She was so different from Bryce but I was reminded of him tonight: her protectiveness, her ease with words and effortless beauty she wore better than the colour red. And the want to fuck her. The way my body begged for her touch.

Suddenly the distance between us was apparent. I patted the bed next to me with a smile that concealed my teeth and puffed my cheeks. She shook her head.

"I should be going."

"No!" Was I that drunk? Was I that utterly drunk that she couldn't come near me? Was I so pitiful she would be taking advantage of me?

My face softened and I only hoped she could see through the results of depleted beer barrels and gin bottles to see what I was really thinking.

I want you. I thought. *Now, on this bed. With the taste of mojitos and chewing gum on our tongue and sounds of giggles on our lips.*

She came and sat next to me with a sigh.

"This isn't right," I said - not what she was expecting.

After speaking about the industry, the annoying and nice, anything but our liking for one other, she was shocked by my abrupt jump to the subject of *us*. She waited for my words. I kissed her instead. She kissed me back. And then she pulled away. This time I waited to see what she would say. But what she did say brought waves of sobriety crashing over me. Made my eyes hot. I felt tears escape them and a lump in my throat that only grew as I tried to keep my eyes on hers.

"Bryce," she had said.

—

Another world
as if he were fiction
a story I could pick up
and continue
then forget when
his pages were closed
but I knew he still could
give me paper cuts

—

She had shown me a world I never knew existed. And then pushed me, instead of the anchor, from the boat as she drifted on. And just like an anchor, I sank to the bottom beneath the waves, screaming for air. It felt like I didn't know which way was up anymore, the waves becoming more vicious around me, knocking and spinning me into no escape. I looked for light as darkness took over my vision. Even if I could see properly what would I look for? The boat? Back to shore where safety awaited me. All I knew was that I couldn't stay beneath the water. Neither here nor there.

I looked up to her, between uncontrollable sobs.

"I think I love you."

She pulled a sad smile and said she knew.

She hugged me until I stopped crying and we found ourselves lying on our backs for a while, looking up at the ceiling, invisibly saying goodbye to inebriation with each sip of water and each hour added to the clock on my bedside table.

We talked for hours about what seemed like everything: what we planned to do after the film, life goals, aliens, art, death, medicine, what flavours of *Oreo* were the best (peanut butter.) She had wiped the tears from my eyes and the ache from my heart with her smooth words of distraction. She made me forget my tiredness until she pointed it out herself. We eventually drifted to sleep and woke late the next day, dehydrated still.

I felt embarrassed when the sun crept through the curtains and woke us. My first thoughts that day were of my sobs and confessions. I felt shame. But no regret. Because I'm sure a few tears escaped her and I'm sure she felt the same way about me. I guess my embarrassment, guilt for Bryce and overall lousiness that morning was just intensified by my massive hangover.

Grace seemed quite content with the morning silence, whilst I found it quite excruciating. I showered. When I came back into the room she had gone.

We didn't speak for days except during scenes at work. Which seemed heavy, laden with our own emotions. I was sure Sasha, with his exceptional observational skills, sensed it all. Confirmed were my thoughts when he pulled us to one side after a few takes to ask if there was anything he needed to know. We agreed to pick up with the scene the next day and I knew it was time to confront her. I couldn't let this get in the way of my work. Grace was eating a peanut butter cupcake in the catering room when I approached her. She smiled a casual smile as if I were merely an extra. As if nothing had happened between us.

"I think we need to talk."

"I agree," she said, in-between her bites of the cupcake and the unsticking of clumps of peanut butter between her teeth, "I was wondering when you'd speak to me." She picked at her teeth with her finger and looked at the remains before placing them back in her mouth. Was I really less interesting than the residue of a cupcake?

I took an apple from the fruit bowl: *Ambrosia*. I took a bite and immediately regretted it. Soft. I felt how a criminal might feel seeing the blue and red flashings of a police car - probably a white collar crime, while I was sure Grace could commit murder and wave the officers by with ease.

"Kora, what *is* the matter?" She interrupted my thoughts of petty crime.

"I don't even know really." Sighs were becoming common in her presence. "I can't concentrate on my lines. Some days I feel so guilty about last week, somedays confused, but mostly I just think about how great it was and hope I didn't fuck it all up. I'm scared people know. I'm wondering if you've told people, I *hate* these apples, but more than anything I just want to know what's going on in your head."

Another sad smile. Sympathy was the last thing I wanted. I suddenly felt myself underwater again, unable to breathe.

"In my head? I'm eating too many cupcakes because the fruit here is shit, trying my best to focus on these stupid lines when you are likely avoiding me, but most of all? Most of all I'm avoiding leaving my hotel room at night for fear of missing a call from your damn room. I'm falling to sleep thinking of you and then thinking how ridiculous I am for spending so much time with you in my head. I've been toying with ringing you while knowing you need space. But obviously that's not working for either of us, so I just need to know if you meant what you said the other night. And I need to know if you plan on acting on it. Because if not, that's fine. And we can shoot this film and do press and stay friends, or never speak again. The ball's in your court. I just can't stay in limbo here… Oh, and Sasha knows something's up."

I was in shock. How could she have kept all of this to herself and masked it so well? She chewed on the last mouthful of cupcake, threw the paper in a bin next to her and walked the table length that was between us.

"But if so, I mean to say, if you *do* plan on acting on it, I just don't want to waste any time not speaking to you any longer… Because I think I love you too." She took my hands with hers.

I was shocked, my throat dry. "You *think*?"

She laughed and tears welled in her eyes. "Are we fucking crazy?"

"I think so." I closed the catering door and kissed her quickly. Then ran back to my trailer, annoyed we hadn't spoken sooner.

I picked up a notepad amongst the stack of books that had travelled with me from England. I tore a page and wrote her a note:

8 pm tonight, don't eat. X

Leaving my trailer, I walked amongst the twinning ones around mine until I saw her name printed and stuck in the window. I folded the paper and pushed it under her door, then spent the rest of the day trying to think of anything but tonight before falling into my taxi at 6 pm.

The mirror was still fogged from my shower. I wiped it with

my towel, blotted some red lipstick onto my lips and flicked black mascara onto my top lashes. My hair had been curled nicely at work, it had fallen throughout the day into soft ringlets that sat on my breasts. No need to wash it. No time to have washed it. I took the elevator from floor five down to two and knocked on door 217.

Breeze

She opened the door. What I saw, where my eyes fell, caused a gulp. She had on a pair of blue jeans, tight, showing a sinuous shape of her body from thigh to neck. And a red strapless top that hugged her chest, the shape of her nipples showing, slightly hard beneath the cotton. Considering the cold temperatures of Salt Lake we were about to stroll through, I was a little shocked.

Her dark skin glowed in the yellow hotel light. She really did look like a movie star. The whites of her eyes glistened around chestnut circles. They oddly reminded me of a puppy's - you couldn't help but love them, be drawn to them despite everything else that was so easy on the eye.

Her teeth, the same white as her eyes, were surrounded by plump, brown, heart-shaped lips, moist in the centre. She had a thin, silver nose ring looped around her right nostril, and was the type to wear such a thing without people noticing unless you looked as intently, and as closely as I, at her face. She noticed my stare and smiled. Grabbing a long red leather coat that reached her ankles, the door flung shut and my grip around her hand tightened as we walked down the corridor to the elevator. The patterned carpet reminded me of that from *The Shining*. And I had the same tickle in my chest that I had when I first watched that film. Was it fear, ecstasy, both? Only Grace could make me feel as if I were living in a movie. I just hoped it ended better than it had at the *Overlook*. Because despite all the exuberance, I always thought of how it would end. All movies came to end after all.

I felt the warmth of her hand, which complemented my always cold palms. The anxiety escaped me. For now.

It was nice to be in control. Not letting go, I led us to the restaurant I'd found during my first night here. It felt like I was sharing this secret with her; this place that nobody knew about except myself and a few locals. It did damn good pizza. That was the only thing I'd ever ordered from the menu, despite returning three times since. I'd fallen so madly in love with the taste of Margherita that I didn't need anything else, didn't *want* to try anything else. Was that what was missing? An infatuation with Bryce so intense that I could never dream of falling for anyone else? Because I knew that tonight, like all other nights, I was going to order the Margherita. Or was I just being completely ridiculous comparing my relationship to a pizza?

***

I was lazily kicking stones around the street a week before now, letting my feet guide me in no particular direction. My only rule being that whatever street I turned to next, I should still see the setting orange fall behind the distant mountains: a contrast to the buildings surrounding me. This is why I fell so quickly in love with Salt Lake. It told me that although I was here alone, without Bryce and the comforts of home, I wasn't so far from the things I loved. When the sun sank below the jagged line in the distance, taking with it the view of the mountains, replaced by bright city lights, I focused my attention on finding food.

I saw a small pizzeria sign amongst bigger, cleaner and brighter ones along a street I thought I'd already walked down earlier that night. Without welcoming doors, others walked by and went elsewhere to satiate their appetite. The sign wasn't neon like the others, but a swinging wooden rectangle hanging over a door that looked like an entrance to an apartment. Upon closer inspection, you could see a piece of paper stuck with blue tack behind the glass displaying *Grigio's* opening times.

I pushed the door and followed two flights of narrowing, creaking stairs up to another entrance where I was met with the smell of fresh basil and garlic which only intensified when I opened the door. This time it was accompanied by a smiling, aged man wearing a greased apron with two wine glasses in hand. He told me to take a seat where it pleased me and that he would soon take my order. I watched his smile leave me and greet the only other people in the restaurant: a couple sat on a round table in the far right corner. They were both in their 60s, easily. The woman wore a green leopard print dress which cocooned her slim body. It showed the little fat she had wrinkled beneath the bra strap, wrapped too tightly around her torso. I felt as if I were invading her privacy. It was minus temperatures outside, her fur coat sat draped over her chair which would usually have covered her entire body should I have seen her outside - she'd worn this dress only for him, her husband. Only him.

Her eyes were only on his as she listened intently to his every word. Their hands sat towered on top of one another in the middle of the table but broke apart when the waiter came and placed the glasses to fill them. The woman briefly met the waiter's eyes - mouthed a 'thank you' - then gave her attention back to her husband. She didn't look my way which made me happy.

I thought of Bryce as I ordered a Margherita from the laminated menu, deciding to ignore the dry splats of food in the corner. The words were surrounded by Italian cartoons. And while I waited, I saw what surrounded me: plastered to the walls were postcards. Some were stuck with the picture facing the wall allowing the intimate messages from 1988, 2000, 1950, to loved ones and family members, to be read by the people of *Grigio's*. I read that Lisa wanted to bring bags of salt back from a man who lived in a cave by the sea of Malta, who made it himself in the salt pans. I read that Cesco was enjoying time with his newborn son in Normandy and that he had sent some polaroids in an envelope that very same day. I read other tales of travel, homesickness, of culture shock and I painted each story in my head, lost in my own imagination until the waiter returned with a steaming pizza that was too large for the plate. It was thin and spread with a generous amount of marinara sauce, huge basil leaves that had been arranged neatly around the middle, almost flower-like, and lastly, oozing dots of mozzarella. The smell of garlic was almost overpowering. *Almost.* It was the best pizza of my life.

***

The same smell met my nose as I led Grace up the stairs. It was a little busier this time, with a small family of four seated where the couple had been before. Still plenty of room and more than enough intimacy for Grace to be as equally impressed as I with the place.

Grace ordered a bottle of red. I pretended to enjoy it for about half a glass until the pizzas came. She then drank my half of the bottle too. By the time we stumbled the streets back to our hotel, stomachs comfortably lined, with each other's arms for support against the snow, Grace was slightly more tipsy than I.

We swung individually through the sliding doors of the lobby. The floor was an immaculate, glossy, black and white patterned marble. It was accompanied by tall ceilings with sparkling chandeliers which, in the daytime, projected rays of a rainbow across the room. There was a fireplace to the right where guests often waited for taxis or read from the bookshelves. The shelves looked almost older than the hotel itself, with stacks of battered books and magazines left by previous guests. In the middle of the room was a black grand piano, equally as polished as the floor.

"I want to play." Her eyes were like a child's at Christmas.

"Grace, it's gone midnight."

She ignored my words and fell onto the velvet red stool perched beneath the keys. It reminded me of the one by our front door, the one Bryce and I had salvaged from the pews. I sighed.

She started playing before I even reached the piano. The stability in her fingers shocked me. Sound oozed around the room as they sank into the keys, flowing as smoothly as those by practised hands around knitting needles. I looked around the lobby and was greeted with a smile from the woman doing the night shift behind reception. She proceeded into a back staff room. We were alone.

Grace changed songs without stopping, each song flowing into the next as if it were one continuous piece. I sat in silence, content with my thoughts until she wove a sound familiar to my ears. For a moment, my excitement gave me the same euphoria she clearly felt while playing. I couldn't remember the song or who sang it but when the time came for lyrics, they fell from my mouth. In the elevator, I realised it had been *New Born* by Muse.

Rain was running against the leather of her coat whilst sinking into the fabrics of mine as I swiped the card key through 217's slot and let her pass in front of me. We left the coats by the door and I picked a CD from her the shelves. I played The Smiths, *The Queen Is Dead* just loud enough to hear.

"This time it's you who needs taking care of." I smirked, eager with confidence.

"I think I'll still be the one taking something tonight."

I felt my cheeks redden, my mind in awe at her ability to still coherently overpower me after a bottle of wine.

I liked it. She wanted to play with my vulnerability, and I was past embarrassment at my want for her. We both knew it, we both knew what was going to happen so I had nothing to lose and nothing to be embarrassed about anymore.

I teased her with the same words she'd spoken to me last week

"I should be going, we can get breakfast in the morning?"

She looked at me for a while and smiled knowingly. I was fighting every urge to walk towards her, kiss her and pull the top from her breasts, unbutton her jeans and slide them down her legs. Instead, I traced her body with my eyes, taking her in. The outfit she had chosen just for me was now mine to look at freely, she puffed her chest slightly when my eyes rested there. Her top, strapless, fell a little as it stretched with her movement. I flickered a glance at her eyes and quickly fell back to her body. Her nipples were hard beneath, the tops of them had creeped from the top - her body almost exposed. I felt a tingle. My body stiffened.

I was wearing mom jeans found second-hand years ago and had worn to death in the winters, along with a thin black turtle-neck. I slid it from my skin slowly, slightly struggling with the tight neck. I almost ripped it from my head. I stood in my jeans and bra staring at her. She was sunk on top of the bed sheets, lying on her side, one hand between her thighs with the other perching her head up. Our gaze remained unbroken as I peeled the socks from my feet - a little wet from the snow that had snuck into my boots. The carpet was thin and hard beneath my feet.

Walking to the door, I turned the main lights off leaving the ones by the bed glowing. She looked beautiful. I softly crawled onto the bed and cradled her; in doing so, she moved from her side onto her back and looked up at me with her hands on my hips. I flicked my hair to one side and leant down to kiss her. She met me half way and we shared a long kiss, our lips barely touching but brushing gently against one another's. My body ached for her now, sat here like this.

Eventually,

I left her lips and moved to her neck, then her shoulders and the dents above her collarbones. I hugged her for a while. I played my fingers over her body as she had done with the piano. I traced the shape of her and heard a noise so sensuous escape in the chord of a moan. I smiled and moved my fingers to her nipple and saw it rise before slipping my hand under the fabric.

———

If her touch were a sound
it would be
the soft crisp crunching of leaves
amongst the silence of the forest
it would be
the glide of fingers
over the finest of silks
the rustle of sheets
masking the natter of morning birds
the delicate crackle of a cigarette
as you inhale its fumes
and see the red dance downwards
chasing your clutched fingers
but what if you still crave more
if the delicacy of silks, cigarettes
leaves and sheets
is not enough
to mask what was before
you might then hope
her touch to be more
like the jab of a needle
the burn of your throat at the passing of whisky
the fading pain of a hit to your hip bone
from the corner of some hidden furniture
like finally pinching a splinter in success
or the breeze floating around the wound
of a scab that you just reopened
opened
opening

- Sacrificial

———

I sat up, perched on top of her, and slipped my second hand under her top. It rose up revealing her round breasts that were now cupped by my grasp: her nipples just visible between the gaps. I squeezed hard. She arched her back and flung her head back, showing the strained muscles in her neck. Her hands pressed hard against me, parting my cheeks. She moved her hands hard over my body, to my thighs, her fingers digging into them, then up to my stomach where she unbuttoned my jeans. She slid the zipper down. I grabbed her hands and pinned them onto the bed. Her nostrils flared with impatience.

We kissed hard this time. I bit and sucked on her bottom lip then further down I ventured. I ripped the jeans from her legs, revealing a laced red thong that sat high on her waist and matched her top perfectly. Lightly, my hands scooped themselves under the fabric sitting on each side of her hips. They made a movement to part the cotton from between her legs.

The darkened mark in the middle saw my teeth biting hard, pulling them upwards. Saliva from my mouth attached to them and turned them darker. Lightly planting kisses between her hip bones I moved to bite the fabric *there.* Where it was already dark. I gently tugged the thong. It all became too much. Frantically, we sat up. In such a rush we were to leave our clothing behind. I stood from the bed and she followed.

In the haste to undress one another, we now stood a few feet apart, taking each other in; the first time we saw each other naked, equally. Her eyes told me before her mouth those three magic words.

"I love you," I replied, biting the skin behind my lip. "And you should know, I've only ever said that to one other person before." A reminder for both of us.

"What about your parents?" she said, inquisitively.

"Well, I never fucked my parents, Grace."

"Right."

silence

"You're so beautiful." Her eyes still on mine.

She smiled and walked to me, cupping my face and kissing me once more. I felt the navel of her stomach touch mine. My eyes stung with heat.

"It's okay." She kissed the tear that slid down my cheeks. It's hard to ignore someone when they cry during sex.

"I don't want to hurt either of you," she spoke slowly, "I don't want to cause any of this."

"No." It was all I could say. It annoyed me that she had spoken of him, even with affection. It only gave me guilt.

"I'd better go you know, I fucking knew I shouldn't have led you on like this. Now look at you."

"Don't speak to me like that." My weak protest.

"Like what?"

"Like a *child*." I pushed her away from me. She paused, shocked by my sudden aggression. We stared at each other, a few feet apart again. Then I grabbed her, harshly pushing her to the wall nearest. We fell into it and she lifted me, my legs wrapping around her. Tangled, we fell onto the bed. My hands were behind her, and then slipping lower, they found her. I slipped inside her and she squirmed in reaction, grinding against me. She looked at me and copied my actions, I copied her moans. That was our language for an hour.

We lay in silence, catching breaths until she took me by surprise.

"I'm in control now." She lifted me from her and flung me onto my stomach. She sat in the arch of my back and I felt her wet against me. She ground on me and I parted my legs in longing.

"Not yet," she whispered as she closed my legs again. It was torture. It made me all the more hungry for her touch, her fingers, her tongue. I grew hot with the quilts against the front of my body and her on my back.

I felt her move so that she was facing my feet. She hit me hard against the cheeks above my thighs.

"Harder," I groaned, again and again.

She grinned and sounded a rhythm with her hits, rapid against me. As she did so, I felt a finger playing, toying with me. She knew my want and laughed before forcing her fingers inside me, quickly now. *Finally.*

And we slept at three.

I reflected on the night as the morning light of Salt Lake City crept into our hotel room. The electronic calendar had been knocked from the nightstand by her bed, I picked it up and saw that we had only two days until we all left for Vegas. I was excited, sad and scared. Just as Salt Lake was becoming home, I was dragged from it. Just like I had been dragged from Bryce, I would soon be in yet another alien place reminiscing on the past.

I turned to see Grace sleeping beside me. Her sleeping body the present, next to me now. I watched her sleep for a while before she woke with a smile and hunger that would soon drag us both out of bed and downstairs to the restaurant for breakfast.

The breakfast buffet was always my favourite at hotels. This time it came only second best to the nights spent with Grace. But it was close. There were rows of food. One displayed different cereals in glass tubes, dispensers at the bottom. Sat next to those was a selection of milks including oat, soy and almond. In an open, coved fridge was fresh fruit: halved strawberries, blackberries, blueberries, pineapple cut into extravagant shapes, orange segments, crips watermelon triangles, all washed and glistening, invited you to top your food with the deep coloured, ripe fruits.

The selection and smell of bread gave me too much decision to make in my sleepy state. There were whole loaves of all kinds: brown topped with pumpkin seeds, oat and cranberry, flat ciabattas stuffed with sun-dried tomatoes and fresh rosemary leaves, round loaves of lemon and poppy seed with candied lemon peel to decorate, and soft, rectangular white loaves dusted with flour. The latter seemed the go-to for toasting. Each labelled with handwritten cards, slotted into wooden blocks. Each equally inviting.

I opted for beans, mushrooms and a few slices of white bread. The most painful part of my morning was watching the slices I had roughly cut travel along the metal racks, under the toaster, and out of the bottom. Once that was over, I could sit contently, watching her eat muesli, wishing we would never grow full and breakfast would never end.

Eventually,

Before I Fall To Pieces

We walked with full stomachs around the city for the last time. We saw the Saturday busy as the locals shopped and tourists scurried with maps in hand. I would miss this view - those mountains serving as a false backdrop. I felt comfort whenever I heard an English accent. I loved Grace's smooth American words but they didn't comfort me like the sound of home could.

After a few hours in the city together, the cold told us to seek warmth back at the hotel. I suggested we pack our rooms together and prepare for tomorrow's departure. Glad for Grace's leading steps towards the elevator were my thoughts, when my own were halted at the doorway of the lobby.

Waiting for me, he must have been watching each person step in and out of the hotel, feeling the cold fly through with each opening. He saw me straight away. My laughter stopped abruptly and left Grace's hanging in the air, alone. She was halfway towards the elevator before she turned to find me, rooted to the ground where I had seen him. Sat on the sofas by the door was Bryce, staring just as intently as I, but for different reasons. While shock and dread filled me all at once, I could see excitement and doting flooding his eyes. My shock granted him an embrace, and tears to hide beneath his shoulder. He smelt good. Like home. I finally raised my arms, and then my head. And by the time I was able to search for Grace, I met her eye as the elevator doors slid and led her back to her room, alone.

"That's Grace." He didn't know.

I nodded my head into his shoulder but said nothing. We spent a few minutes just holding each other, trying to erase the month spent apart.

"I've missed you so much," I whispered, nose sniffling.

"Don't." He squeezed my arms before releasing me and asking if we should go to my hotel room. It was only as the key was in the door that fear filled me - the possibility that something of Grace's might be in my room. At first glance, there was nothing of hers. But my angst persisted. I could smell her. I think he could sense something too, scanning the room. He ignored whatever grudge he had and picked up my copy of *The Shining* that had been swat onto the floor in frustration some nights before, where creases had surely now sunk permanently into the pages.

"Your favourite." He slid his long fingers over the pages, trying to flatten the creases.

Whatever he tried to do, the pages sprung back to the damage done by my recklessness. Again, I thought of Grace and knew that what I'd done couldn't be smoothed. A dent remained in the story.

"What's going on Kora?"

There was never going to be a right time to tell him. Never the right words to soothe the pain that would surely come. All I knew was that if I delayed telling him, it was even more of a betrayal. I took a deep breath and hugged him. Hugged him like I had never hugged him before. Hugged him for what I was sure would be the last time, with my heart full of emotion and muscles tensed. I exhaled and let go of him. I exhaled and let him go.

——

I tried to feel strong
waiting for my next collapse
I could touch him forever
I could caress
sail my fingers
over the waves
of him
if only
I hadn't already done so
with her

——

"Fuck Bryce, *fuck*." His face dropped. His mouth silent, waiting.

"I never thought you'd come here." *Why did you come now? Why couldn't you let me live this selfish fairytale and have you await me at the end, upon my return?*

"And why is that bad?" I could see anger flecking him, like fear often did my vision when the church was without him.

"I thought you would know when you saw her - saw *us*. Or you'd find out from the news or something. Fuck, I thought it would ease me into this. I thought you'd shout at me and push me and tell me I'm nothing, that I'm selfish and stupid." I sank onto the edge of the bed while he stood by the door, still, arms crossed. In a quieter voice, I spoke now, relieved, for some reason.

"Now I'll watch that look you give me fade to disappointment. And that's the worst. I'd rather anything but your disappointment Bryce. Always." I saw it happen then.

"Who?" he croaked. His lipped tense and curled inwards.

...

"Grace"

———

Each name
did the same
in the presence
of the other

———

He now faced a decision harder than the choice of bread at breakfast. He had flown all the way here to find his relationship in the dirt, *soggy*. Did he stay and work things out or leave? Seek space which he'd already spent so much time with this month? It was all on him, and yet he gave me that, too:

"So what do you want to do?" I hated how good he was.

"Me?"

"You." A smirk. How was he smirking? How was his charm not lost on me in the midst of all of this? I questioned whether he'd feel the same if Grace were a boy.

"I don't know. I need time, I need to think."

"It's simple Kor, who do you love?" He was serious now. Keeping his distance still, waiting for the verdict.

"I love you both." I exhaled. "But I think I love her more."

I told him and broke his heart before we could work things out. He sank to the floor, claiming my hotel room, telling me I must leave him be, and go to her as I had chosen. I knew he tasted sorrow then, while I tasted salty tears that swam into my mouth. I knew that in those words, I couldn't have him again. I had to get out before I regretted my decision. I left everything with the croak of a 'sorry' in that hotel room. I ran to her room, she was there in an instant. I fell into her arms sobbing uncontrollably, screaming incoherent words. She said nothing but words of comfort. She simply waited for calm. It came in the night. We fell to sleep then, with a kiss - the first that failed in my forgetting of the other.

Eventually,

Falling For Grace

We drove for miles on what seemed like our own roads, the valley around us dry with heat. I looked up. The whites against the blue were beautiful. I became mesmerised, following the outlines of the clouds with my eyes. Seeing each curve, each part of cloud that was defined and then others that sank into softer lines and merged with the sky, like water diluting paint. I wondered what they felt like. I imagined quite cold. And wet.

The sun was setting, we were chasing those clouds into an a great, merged evening yellow shape. A shape quite like ocean waves. But instead of sand castles stood palm trees. Instead of fish flew birds. Instead of goggles, we wore the windshield between us and the sky.

We had hired a car for the day to get from Salt Lake to Vegas, while the rest of the crew flew. Extras were local to the city so we would meet a whole new bunch of them in Vegas. Grace insisted we hire the most ostentatious car possible: a 1970 Ford Mustang convertible, glossy red. We drove with the top down and the music loud as she talked enthusiastically about music which made me think of Bryce, momentarily. It had been a tough day, but driving now I felt better. I was finally beginning to know I had made the right choice. *Choice.*

The pain was numbing now.

We drove and drove. Through traffic, then desert, until the

roads became our own and the top of the car had to be lifted for heat. I didn't ask where we were, I didn't think it was important. I'd learnt about cars from being on the road with Bryce, amid band crew and friends. We were squeezed into their double-decker tour bus, going city to city, show to show and bar to bar through the previous two Septembers. I now found his words mimicked as I spoke them to Grace, passing through the corners of Arizona to the border of Nevada.

I was glad her eyes were on the road. It gave me chance to look at her. At those glossy arms stretched to hold the wheel, the profile of her jawline, as sharp as her turns in the road. Occasionally I would look up at the sky and become lost like she did when she spoke of music and film. The bright, white clouds against the blue reminded me of renaissance paintings you might see on the ceilings of chateaus. I watched her eyes bulge and saw life in the stories she told me, her memories flashing through her mind and escaping through her expressions and tone. She was madly in love with Tame Impala.

"First album is ok, but this one is a masterpiece. There's no other way to put it, really." She injected the CD into the player and turned the volume up. Where I had packed my suitcase full with books, she'd filled hers with CDs. I wanted to like it. I wanted to see what she saw in them. I sat in silence, listening to the lyrics sung by an echoed voice over piano and guitar. We sat in a serene silence until the car played *Eventually* and she told me it was the greatest breakup song of all time. She told me to listen to the lyrics.

The only thing I truly heard in those three minutes were of how it felt like murder to put someone's heart through this. Whatever *this* was, I thought the singer and I shared something in common.

I didn't know anything about how any of us should feel. But I'd made up my mind for sure, listening to Tame Impala, with the woman I knew I loved by my side. She turned to smile at me as the song ended as if to say 'I told you so'. I smiled back at her and placed my hand on hers, above the gear stick. She glanced down before returning her eyes to the road. I thought I saw another smile creep along her face. I was happy.

Eventually,

—

The wind curves in and out
of creases around my ear
it paints a picture
and tickles my skin
but no feeling more tickling
and soothing
than her hand tracing mine
causing adrenaline
to knock on hearts door
and welcome him like an old friend
and run a marathon
around my veins

—

She insisted on dropping me at our new hotel before taking the car back to the rental place. I protested but she won and so found myself alone in our room after a perfect day, reflecting on the elation that infected me.

Today had been a confirmation of what I suspected. I still knew so little about her but I was somehow ok knowing that I would likely find out soon. I wanted to know her favourite wine, her hobbies, what her childhood was like, her insecurities. I wanted to know the woman that I had fallen for, but I also knew that with each new discovery would come increasing guilt, despite my honestly with Bryce. I wasn't a cheater, but in most moments since our first night together, I knew what it felt to be one. To hold a secret your partner had every right to know. For despite letting go of Bryce I still felt the more time I gave to her, the more betrayal I gave to him. I just couldn't win.

Her Spell

We packed our bags separately
and unpacked them together
said goodbye to introductions
and hello to slot machines
and miniature European landmarks
which didn't seem small at all
but reminded me
that in a months time
the sound of shutters would wake us
telling us the rest of the world has woken
and the Italian sun would grace our skin
with gifts of bronze
if only my thoughts of him
felt as good as the changing of my pigments
maybe being that close to home
would just remind me
of my ghoulish complexion
which had served me perfectly
before I left

It had taken only two weeks for us to decide to share a room. We agreed that when it came to Vegas we'd request only one. It felt like a new chapter for me. In my head, I called it *Her Spell.* Because that's exactly what I was under. Almost all of my time was spent thinking of her, looking, admiring. And I wasn't ashamed. *Shame is very different from guilt*, I thought. And I was not ashamed of the love I was so heavily bound to.

Anchored.

The film crew were feeling more like family with each day that passed. The belief that Del Ponzo had given me in casting me in his film would be something I'd never forget. In a way, he was the gateway to my success in film and TV, but also to Grace.

Salt Lake was so full of new beginnings that Vegas was actually a relief, a settlement. A place where I selfishly thought less of Bryce by succumbing to Grace. It felt like a weight lifted from my shoulders. To have the confidence to leave him for her. What I did wasn't right. But we all make selfish decisions in life. We have to in order to feel happy. But should we spend time moping with regret and guilt? Because if so then the decision itself is a wasted one.

The only worries I really had in Vegas were those of press coverage. With interest in the film growing, more pictures were being taken, more security being added to ensure everyone on set was meant to be there. I worried whether a picture would be tomorrows headlines: *'Grace Winter and her new love interest'.* I just didn't want Bryce to have to see that. I still cared for him and knew what that would do to him.

Two weeks in, I woke early. I guess the early starts had finally inhabited my sleeping pattern. Careful not to wake Grace I dressed into a sports bra and leggings. I left the room with only a water bottle and room key in hand, which slotted nicely into the inner of my leggings. I wasn't sure where I was going but the day was mine. I ran for miles. As if running would undo the cigarettes I'd consecutively smoked on the balcony last night with her.

Happily listening to others on balconies above us—getting gradually louder as more drinks were presumably poured—is where we spent our evening. The air was cool, with little breeze. It made for a much nicer balcony environment than Salt Lake had. Though Grace was only five years older than I, it showed when we spoke of films. It exuded her so strongly you might question whether it was just her time as an actress in the film industry where she'd got it from. It was as if her whole life had always been centred so passionately around film. It wasn't just the performances in which she was so enthusing of, which us like minds usually focused on, but the lighting, sound score, the grading. The technicals, the cameras used. Everything. She knew it and spoke of it well. All gushing from her I wondered whether she loved me like she did film.

Though it didn't intimidate me, nor deter me. This word of mouth was the best kind of education one could get, I thought. To learn about films I hadn't yet seen, and why I should. To go to parties with Sasha and the others, speak to the top tier of the hierarchy about film. I think I learnt more there than I ever did at film school. Though utterly disgusted she was, and fractionally embarrassed was I, when she heard I was still to watch some of the classics. I simply said I made up for it with my taste in what I *had* seen. And attempted to give something to the conversations with the film superiors I found myself tangled with at those parties.

"You're going to go far, you know," she remarked, after listening to my doting on a few Kubrick classics, amongst my more modern infatuation with Lanthimos. The conversation had continued in the taxi from another film party, and out to the darkness of the balcony one night in Vegas.

"Really?" I could never take a compliment, especially when I knew it was genuine.

"I mean it. The way you are on set shows it alone. But, I mean, it's the way you speak about film. The way you go a little red when you can't always speak what you're thinking. As if words couldn't quite do justice to that of which you're thinking. It's really beautiful to have a conversation with you."

"Thank you. That means a lot. Sometimes it's hard speaking to people at those parties. I so easily lose my train of thought, or forget myself mid-sentence because my mind becomes side-tracked on another part of my story. But I feel like with you it's so easy."

"It is." She passed me her cigarette after blowing the ash towards the darkness beyond the railings.

"You really get me."

There was a shout from above, which diluted any chance of tears with the sleep of my eyes.

I diluted the toothpaste with my spit
it foamed and did the same
with the water down the drain
I fell into your bed
no our bed
let it ease the pains
let them sift through my blood
and my veins
giving them rest
when the covers scrunch less
rest from the mess
the exhaustion you give
the cigarettes you lit
so then I can wake
and let more fumes dilute their way
down to my lungs
watch each other's pupils dilate
ready for another together kind of day

-Alkaline

There was an apocalyptic mood to the early hours of Vegas, with the odd cluster of drunken men stumbling back to their hotel, wishing for the darkness to remain so their night could continue. It was by no means quiet, just quiet*er*. Wherever I was in the world, I felt a connection to the people I saw on the streets during those early hours, whilst everyone else slept. We were the few to have risen for the day. We had the head start.

It was rather a lot more run-down than I imagined Vegas, the place of movies, to be. Maybe because I was viewing it in its entirety as the sun overpowered the glow that usually surrounded the building at night and hid decay. Without that neon glow, it all felt a little foreign. And bigger, much bigger.

Change Of The Seasons

He was the winter of my life, and she - my summer. I preferred each in their own time. In the winter he often toured. But when he didn't we burned fires to keep warm at night, drank from flasks that kept our hands as well as our insides warm on walks over mountains, each step closer to a new blister.

And those cold months of touring, I was always by his side; watching side stage, seeing fans want exactly what I had. Or seeing others care a little less about the persona and more about what he created; dancing and screaming the words of his songs into the faces of their friends, plastic cups in hand.

What we had at night after his shows were squeezed into a single bed on the tour bus until we glimpsed his name lit up at the next venue. Where there were usually fans already queueing as we were ushered inside.

I watched him tell crowds how special they were, imitating the same script the following nights to others. He sang songs to the thousands that he'd first only sung to me in the comforts of our home, watching the fire crackle.

Sometimes I might leave through a side door into the crowd, to feel how I used to in my teenage years. I truly had the best of both worlds mimicking his words, unnoticed and lost in those crowds, ignoring the few close enough, or caring enough, to notice the 'AAA' pass stuck to my leg or wristband, telling others I *knew* him.

The short days and long nights collaborating with his career meant for a deep love of the darkness. But what should happen when I left the darkness of English winters?

Summer brought with it a new adventure, a new exploration of places you couldn't go in winter. Longer days, shorter nights. Of dehydration being our only motive to move our sunken bodies from the sand by day, and the cold that would finally catch us as we swam in rivers of Italy by night. And trips to the arcade, where our pockets were lined with loose change that got lighter with each drop of a coin. Where joy would rush through us when we'd get some of our own money back, for it meant we could spend a few more moments under those fluorescent lights and cheap prizes that we so desperately desired. We would laugh at our misfortune feeling no less poor of an experience. We would walk on to the next arcade and exchange more cash for laughs and memories I would later look at and adore.

I couldn't say who I loved more. You see, the two were incomparable. You might think you love Summer more until you're stifling in the waves of heat you can see before the windowsill. You might crave winter until you forget your gloves in an evening stroll through the snow. Then what are you left with? That familiar craving for the new season. A readiness for change - maybe I shouldn't have ever left England for the climate of America.

Bryce and I had driven a million miles down a road of lust, excitement and unconditional love for two years. He was all I needed, I never wanted more than him. But *more* insisted on fogging my mind, on giving me the ultimatum I hated having. I could not live with one and the other in unison. I could only love one. And it was the hardest decision of my life - to put my brain in control of my heart.

I don't think that's what I did.

Back To Reality

When she wakes
I know I am alone
she's the kind of hidden demon
that can burn me down
I took her with me in my suitcase
I had no say
but she said she loved me
that no one could fuck me
the way she did when we were all alone
usually at night
when I craved sleep
to take my sight
but I saw her fighting him off

when she speaks up
they think I'm on my own
they don't know they'll never really know
she might not be real
she never really will be
but she could kill me
she will fuck me
until I am six feet deep
she will make it seem sweet

make me believe
that all this time
I wasn't crazy
I'm crazy I always will be
and thats just me and thats just me and that is just me

the kind of love that nobody else can see
this drug is so easily taking me
it hurts to breath and I can feel my heart beats

the kind of love that I cannot live without
the kind of love I fucking hate I can't get out

I can see bones see bones see my bones
she loves me best when I'm hungry
she fucks me best when I'm moody
she is invisible
to people
outside

- My head

—

I'd had nothing but a salad, the craving for more than four hours sleep, a bottle of iced tea and four cigarettes all day: the perfect cocktail for a hangover replica. I was being driven back to the airport and felt relieved of the language barrier between myself and the taxi driver, in no mood for light conversation, in no mood to crease my skin into a false sense of happiness.

The silence left my mind to wonder upon the mess that awaited me at home. I played out a hundred different scenarios in my head but they all ended the same: with me leaving. All the work we'd done, the love we'd put into making the church our own. Soon it would all be his with so much of myself etched into the walls, the carpet, the bed. How could I do this to him? My eyes watered and I fought against blinking because I knew tears would fall. I didn't want that as an engagement for conversation. Instead, I turned and stared out of the window and before I knew it we were parked in the terminal drop off, I was closing the door of the taxi, grabbing my own luggage from the boot, eager to leave this country despite knowing what was awaiting me in England.

The flight was delayed. Of course, it was. Eventually, I got a window seat and tried to stay present. To simply watch the city get smaller as I flew higher, thinking of nothing but who was driving those small dots of lights along those stretches of road below.

It was a night flight, two hours from Milan to London. When I could no longer see the blue, red, white cracks of the city, I opted for music as a distraction. Something calming seemed fitting with those drifting to sleep around me. Though I think Rage Against The Machine was a closer depiction of my mood and mind, the directions I was trying to distract my mind from steering towards. But trying to replicate the calm around me I settled with the strings of Cohen, and finally unwound my thoughts into nothingness. Surrounded by the dark of the aeroplane, I felt completely alone. And for the first time in a while, that felt good. Every now and then I looked out of the window, wondering where we were, whether people below could see the lights of our aeroplane, who they were, in those speckled dots of light below, until my eyes closed and I drifted to sleep too.

It felt good to stretch my legs. I often enjoyed the long walk from the plane to passport control. And then from the airport to my car in the multi-storey car park. England greeted me with heavy midnight rain. I drove wishing there were four more gears to drive me into nonexistence. Though the weather was tempting that desire too easily: driving in the fastest lane, I flashed past peoples reduced speeds in mists of water. My car skidded over puddles, halting the cruise control. And my bonnet was hit with waves of rainwater from the other side of the road where southbound drivers were speeding much the same as I. I questioned their recklessness. What caused a sense of urgency so much to risk death behind the wheel? I knew mine.

Three hours left, two, two and a half, one hour…

I was in a tired haze that told me I shouldn't be driving, reconfirmed when the squeak of wipers against the dry windscreen squealed in protest, telling me the rain had stopped long ago. I flicked them off, turned my music up and opened my window for some fresh air. *Diet Mountain Dew.* I loved that song. Then it made me think of Salt Lake. I changed to the radio and caught the end of *Paris Latino* - too upbeat.

My wheels spun another 40 miles as a deep orange fought off the purple of the night. A little while later that morning light shone into my eyes through the side mirrors, startling the tiredness out of me. It hurt to look back. But I welcomed the pain. Pain was what I knew would soon be a common association to my memories with Bryce.

My feet were heavy with dread, my shoulders too from the bags hauled over them. I sighed and unlocked the door.

—

I saw
an ashtray
cans
last nights clothes
all covering the place
where we had once called
our home

—

He was drunk. Really drunk. He'd also been smoking inside which we'd always agreed not to do. But what could I do? It wasn't my home anymore…was it? His state angered me before I pitied him. My arms yearned to wipe the tears from his eyes. I almost forgot everything to tell him everything was alright and that I wouldn't leave and that this was all just a bad dream. But I couldn't. I had to do what my heart had been telling me to do since the first day I'd met her. I was confused and frightened, but most of all disappointed in my inability to please everybody.

Bryce had been my first love. This could be the biggest regret of my life, but I couldn't stay here for fear of leaving. I couldn't stay and question myself for the rest of my life. Better to destroy what I had and know that what I did was right at the time, than to cower away, ignore my feeling and confusion and have it ingrained in my head every time I thought of her. I'd made up my mind and I had to go through with it. No matter how much it hurt me now.

I knew people would judge me. For unearthing what was outwardly a perfect life. The house, the man, the job. All to… *experiment?* I knew that's what my mum would say, Tilda too. I could barely understand it myself. It's not like I'd grown bored of him, or that the thrill had gone. And that's what made it harder; we truly were perfect for each other. But if I had the same feelings towards another, how could I ignore that? I had to do something, and somehow, despite the pain, this felt right.

"Bryce."

His glazed eyes turned to me, head lulling.

"There you are." He smiled. A rush of guilt flooded me as if his tippled state was my doing.

Instinctively I forgot my bags at the door and rushed to kneel on the floor to face him. I cushioned his face with my hands which he leaned on for a while before abruptly pushing them away.

"No, get away." He threw his head back against the sofa and rubbed his face messily with his hands.

"Look what you've done to me." He pointed at his face and blinked a few tears from his eyes.

"Two months of *nothing*. And annoyingly, she's amazing. She's perfect for you." Though his tone suggested sarcasm, I heard only truth in those words. "Maybe even more so than me. Maybe that's why you need to leave."

Silence.

I love you, I'm sorry, I love you. "Bryce." It was all I could say.

Eyes closed, he just smiled, tears rolling beautifully down his face, his speech unaffected.

"I was so fucking angry when I left Salt Lake, you know. Fuck, it killed me." He laughed as if his anger in Salt Lake had been wrong in some way. He laughed not in vain, not sarcastically, but that lovely laugh he did, genuine. I loved him for it.

"Don't swear, you're in church." The juxtaposition of a smile met the tears on my cheeks like birth in a morgue.

Even after everything we were just the same, we never argued. Even as I watched his heartbreak, we were still fine. We could still laugh. We smiled at each other and sat in silence on the cold church floor. We knew I had made up my mind, he knew I would soon leave. We kissed. He told me he loved me and he forgave me and that he understood, though I don't think he really did.

I'd never seen alcohol leave somebodies system as quickly as that night. Sad, considering alcohol was often a dependency for those with heartbreak. And all I could think was whether he would be this understanding if I'd fallen for another man.

He stroked my arm: a silent reassurance that he was ok. His touch got lighter along my body until it was a tickle. Touching me now, the same as he always had. I tried to tell him we shouldn't do this, but I *wanted* him. I kissed him hard, hoping that it would tell him how much I still loved him. That he still meant everything to me, that there never would be another like him. He messily lifted my skirt and squeezed me.

He kissed me lower and lower until I was pressing his head against me, fingers gripping his curls. I sank to the floor. He joined me, keeping his clothes on but unzipping his jeans. He ripped the skirt from my legs and then my thong, my bum bare against the cold concrete. No tears left him now, but there was intent in his eyes. We both knew this was the last time we would fuck. It made me want him more. He turned me over, my hip bones hard against the floor, his hands holding mine in place, pinning them flat against the concrete. He squeezed them hard; the pain felt good. Thrusting against me, my skin scraped the concrete. He quickened and our bodies made noise as they clapped together faster and faster until we were finished. He quickly left me laying on the floor to shower. I turned over and saw blood trickling from the bones of my waist. It stung more somehow, now I saw it. I heard him cough whilst I lay growing colder with each minute unsure of what I had done.

I stayed the night, giving myself time to collect and load my belongings into the Jeep. He had fallen asleep on the sofa and left me to sleep alone in the bed. That hurt. I left him alone and climbed the crooked stairs, admiring each step we had refurbished together. I thought of us sitting for hours doing cheap handiwork until I moaned so much that Bryce would lift me away from the tools and onto the bed, or the kitchen side while he made tea.

It looked like he had already started packing for me.

I still saw this room as ours. My epitome of comfort. Where I found sleep easiest and early starts hardest. To prise myself away from that room and leave him had only ever been a small bane when I knew I'd be returning again at night. But this time I had neither the comfort of him by my side nor the knowledge that I would return. And with that, I found sleep the hardest. The last night in my bed.

—

I lay
until laying hurt
water left my right eye
mascara ran into the pillow
until the blinds were closed
the music on the tv stopped
a new film started
everyone had gone
the smell of their food too
until time became a mystery
I regretted how my body
succumbed to exhaustion
and confused me
I lay

—

I came into the living room to find him sat watching TV, cigarette in hand. A cup of tea sat side by side with the ashtray: steam and smoke rising in unison. Ash dropped carelessly onto the concrete, just missing the rug that sat under the coffee table. He hadn't made me one.

"Do you mind?" I lifted the kettle in asking so. I thought now it might be unfair to still treat this as my home.

He briefly left the TV to look at me.

"Yeah, yeah." He was just so blasé.

I filled the french press. Extra powder. I loved that smell. I didn't bother with milk or sugar. Didn't want to sift through his cupboards, see what he'd been eating. On second thought, I didn't really want the coffee anymore. I ran from the room, urgency giving me strength to carry more weight to my car.

I left twenty minutes later, not how I imagined. We barely spoke that morning and all I can really remember is how little he looked at me. His was of coping. I never thought that might be the last time I saw Bryce. I should have never said goodbye like that.

The Church Inn

—

I sat in the pub
the one by our house
on that quiet street by the railway crossing
with frozen chips
and sachets of sauce
with cold toilets
that made me feel the warmth when I left
from the fire
the same
as the one in our house

—

We ate salt and vinegar crisps here. We talked and laughed with the old locals who had their regular seats around the room. Through the alcove to my left led into a small room taken up by a pool table and rack of old cues of different sizes. There were still holes in the ceiling where I had, on numerous occasions, punctured with my cue in light anger at my defeat, to which the owner had always laughed off while his Jack Russell had run to collect the falling dust with his tongue.

It felt wrong coming here alone as if the place had turned sad in our absence - or my presence, alone. I finished my drink and left with a goodbye to a girl I did not know behind the bar. I took one last look at the outside, with its beautiful brickwork and arched doorway, and the windows that were so poxy you might question why they were there. So much character deserved to hold such memories. I didn't think I would ever return here, so I smiled and turned my back on another one of my favourite places.

—

It's just funny that I see
nostalgia with unfamiliarity
in the strangers who sit upon stools
as wobbly as their sobriety
just like we did

- A perfect contradiction

—

How I wished for video over dvd
with its manual winding
after abruptly ending
with the screen turning to black
as I lay blocking the credits from my eyes
to take a nap my body begged for
having to reach for the remote
to stop the music and its questions
on repeat
asking for you to play
to start or to watch

—

I moved to London with Grace. She already had a place there where she stayed 6 months of the year, her other half spent in Los Angeles. I wondered whether we would go there together while driving Southbound towards my new home. Three hours, two service stations and ten minutes of standstill traffic.

Bittersweet was a taste I'd grown accustomed to these past two months. I only hoped I could grow to like it, the same as a child grew to love that bittersweet flavour of coffee.

I was glad when I saw her. She greeted me at my car with a hug from behind and felt the weeps spasm my body.

"It's over now, you've done your best." She handed me a parking permit to place on the dashboard of the Jeep.

I hung my Dali prints taken from the church, which fit in well with Grace's trinkets. And finally, I exhaled. The last of the bags had left the boot. I breathed in the evening air of Notting Hill. Suddenly I felt a rush of happiness warming my body. Looking around at the curving row of Victorian, pastel coloured houses, surrounded by trees, and a bus stop two doors down, I knew I was truly happy here. Back in London. No matter how much the country would mean to me now, here had been my home before I knew that life. I knew I had made the right decision now. And that made me smile.

English Breakfast

Sometimes my evening cravings were of coffee
moments before sleep
sometimes my mornings were those of tea
sometimes I think
what if I had the instincts of others
reached for what was right
in the back of the cupboard
what if I had lived passively
and drank my coffee in a morning
tea at night
            what if
we fought the same
would something else
have pulled the trigger justly
but with my mind
I can't help wondering
and wondering
about the faults
things so stupid
like putting the blame
on English Breakfast tea

Three months later

With Semi-Skimmed

"Do you want a coffee?" The palm of my hand pressed downwards on the cafetière.

"What milk is there?"

It was a sunny day in London. The light striking in from the window made her only a dark silhouette, a dark shape peeping above the sofa.

"Soy."

Our living area was open plan, I was in the kitchen area so she had no trouble hearing me above the droning noises from the TV - background noise.

"Ew." Should I have be stood where the sun was shining, I'd have seen wrinkles line her nose then.

"I'll take that as a no then." But I didn't need to be stood there to know the face that usually always accompanied that tone.

...

"What is it?" And she didn't need to see me to know I was pissed. We knew each other well, I'll give us that much.

"Nothing, Grace." *Drop it Kora, drop it.*

"Well, it's obviously something." *She's testing you, swaying a rod with bate. Well, don't swim today, don't bite - are you hungry?*

"As if you don't know."

"No actually, I don't." She turned from the TV to face me, her body still a shadow.

"Ok, let's do this." I threw the spoon onto the kitchen side and turned to her.

"Do what?"

"I think I need to just tell you everything I'm not happy with right now."

"Everything?" I'd never realised how much I disliked sniggers. How patronising they were. It annoyed me.

"And I think you need to tell me everything I do that annoys you too." *Smart words, well done Kora.*

"Fuck this," she dismissively muttered as she got up to leave.

"Sit the *fuck* down," I screamed.

We stared at each other for a moment, both in shock. My eyes were beginning to acclimatise to the light. Her eyes were just becoming visible now.

"All I'm saying is, I don't want a coffee if all we have is soy milk." There was a crack in her voice now. *Finally*, I thought, *I'm getting through to her.*

Or maybe… *Finally*, I thought, *I'm hurting her.*

I laughed.

"I think you need to stop being so sensitive."

"No. I think I need to leave." I left her blank faced in the living room.

———

The conversations
aren't the same
the disagreements
more frequent
the laughter
more strained
I think we've changed
while our growth
has been stunted

———

All of the reasons why I had fallen in love with her still shadowed us. But the light around those shadows was so beautiful and much easier to look upon. Why was I squinting into the shadows, as I had just been doing, trying to find the emotions on her face when I could see so easily where the light lay.

I didn't believe in ghosts. And I sure as hell wasn't going to stick around for memories of what were now dead.

I franticly pulled a suitcase from under our bed and started throwing my things into it.

"Why"? She stood in the doorway, no emotion to her voice. I didn't look at her, just carried on packing.

"Why are you doing this? I love you." A little more panic now. Maybe she realised I was serious.

"Stop this." She tried to grab the clothes from my hands.

"Get off Grace, I'm done."

"How has it come to this? You're being so dramatic."

"Well, maybe you shouldn't have an actress for a girlfriend." I stormed into the bathroom, slammed the door and started throwing toiletries into another bag.

Silence

I sat on the toilet seat, breathing deep. In, out, in, out. I felt dizzy. Was I really doing this all over again? My life felt like one big mess. Had it all been a mistake after all? Was she right, was I just being dramatic? I sat until the questions stopped flowing and my heartbeat slowed.

When I finally lifted myself from the toilet, I headed back to the bedroom and zipped up my case. Grace had gone, the TV still on mute.

I needed procrastination. I didn't feel stable enough to drive, so I dug a pen and notebook from my handbag and sat at the dining table. I spoke to her for the last time through a letter:

Grace,

Remember when we first met? That first day on set? I couldn't keep my eyes off of you. I remember you wore that Colorado jumper. I've taken it, I hope you'll forgive me.

And that red top, the strapless one. God, that night. I think that's when I knew. I knew from that moment that I had to be with you.

I still love you. I will always love you. I just have to go. Love isn't enough. We argue, we ignore each other, we deliberately piss each other off. I don't think it's the same kind of love we had at first. We got used to each other and I think it turned into this habitual love. Lazy, almost. And I don't want to stay just for the sake of it. I can't.

You tested me time and time again and I overreacted. I think we did this to ourselves but just like before, I'm being the brave one and stepping away.

I want you to know that I will always remember the times we spent together. Hell, they might haunt me for the rest of my life. But it was all worth it. Salt Lake, Vegas, Verese. The most confusing and exciting times of my life were those spent with you.

I should remember to thank Sasha one day, I fucking miss that guy.

I need time to think things through. Please give me the space I need. I know I'm being a drama queen but I need this time to figure out where my happiness lies. And then I shall follow.

Goodbye, for now, my love

Eventually,

—

Are you waiting?
waiting for me too?
waiting for me to…
well join the queue
I am waiting
and it's agony
to put myself through
who do I choose
what a luxury
what a tragedy

—

Three months. That's all it took for time to grow envious of our happiness. And like a jealous schoolboy, he crept. He whispered, encouraged the clouds above us to grow fat, plump and greedy from our seemingly endless love. Until finally, they grew so large and dark that there left no room for light, only rain and gusts of wind that blew between us. Until we were both too cold to comfort one another. Until we spent our evenings alone, in separate rooms. Or instead, satisfied our emptiness with words as cold as the clouds, until we left scars upon the fonder memories of one another.

I'm not sure whether I fell out of love with her then, after those three months, but we started to argue more and more as time did his dirty work. As if he were continually famished and quenching his thirst on our love, or feeding on popcorn as he watched us crack. The nights were filled with petty fights or backhanded comments about our living habits, political opinions or artistic preferences. I thought of Bryce more and more each day and yet again found the pressure of the media too much. Often paparazzi stood on our road in a morning. Maybe not even waiting for us, but I felt the pressure to look happy nonetheless. For being watched only heightened my anxiety in public. I started going out with her less each day, with a plastered smile upon my face, until I had to leave. I had to get away from London, from the media and from Grace. It wasn't easy, but it was easier than it had been with Bryce. Maybe because I was doing it for the second time. Maybe because I knew it would be the last. The last time breaking somebodies heart. I'd spent the past month reminiscing on those hotel memories in Salt Lake, Vegas and Italy. Reliving the favourites in my head and falling in love with her all over again, then for it to be shattered by reality when she walked through the door. I had taken the courage from somewhere to leave Bryce when he had loved me most, so I hoped leaving Grace when her love was nothing more than a stagnant, habitually festering romance would be easier.

———

Smoke
hovered around her teeth
watered her eyes
salty and warm
urged by sadness
and helped by heat
of the cigarette
to leave her eyes
just like
I would leave her

———

I wondered where my life would take me. Which days of the present would become memories I would cherish, and which would I forget? I think that if I could have boxed them up amongst my most prized possessions, those first meetings with both Bryce and Grace would be slotted nicely amongst my old festival wristbands and handwritten letters from loved ones. The days in the mud, by the stage, in the cold of the church during the move in. And with Grace, the first night we ate Italian together, the road trip to Vegas, the month spent in Italy where we shared a room, as well as our status with the rest of the world. I hoped I could simply throw away these past few months, or at least, put them in a box with the things I rarely thought about - like the smell of those toilets at the festivals.

I hoped. I had hope. Hope.

Eventually,

part two
the breakdown

Eventually,

—

Follow me he said
from behind
come outside he said
from inside
trust me he said
as he lied
I'm staying here he said
as he turned
I did everything he asked
knowing his past
for the ride

—

Interval

I remembered more than I thought I did. The squared patterns on the tiles, the sanguine umbrellas dampening in luminescent, sticky cocktails that would soon dampen our night with petty arguments between my mother and father. But this time nobody was here. At least, I didn't think so. Until I heard mother's voice call my name. It woke me from the sheets still tucked stubbornly under the bed corners by the maid. I remember Linda, the maid, rather well ever since Mother shouted at me after I accused her of taking my flip flops. Flip flops that were likely five sizes too small, upon reflection. I'd soon found them under my bed in line with my other shoes and so, after a violent cry of apologies to Mother, a tradition of tipping her the remains of my holiday money thereafter was made.

Her voice was distant, it left the thoughts of Linda and lifted my feet from the bed. It urged me, fear in chest, feet bare, towards her sound. But the closer I got to that homely familiarity, the warmer I got. It spread through my usually cold hands and feet, apprising me to my surrounding. *How did I actually get here?* I hadn't been here in 15 years. I turned to look at the bedroom of my childhood summers. A sad nostalgia smirked at me in the shapes of those thin bed sheets, in the cold of the floor and the heat of my feet. It all felt wrong.

I walked into the bathroom in a heated discomfort. With a

ticking, the extractor fan blasted to life. I sat on the toilet seat and urged my body to relieve itself. Yet, with my bladder so heavy against my stomach, nothing came except pain. I stood from the toilet and turned the tap so as to at least relieve my body of the sweat pulsing from my pores. But from the hot or cold of the lime green plastics exerted any water. I growled and flung myself up to face my reflection in the matching green-lined mirror.

Horror struck me and ripped a hoarse sound from my throat. It looked as though I'd fallen into the mantelpiece of my parent's house, where pictures sat in slightly more modern frames than that of the mirror in this old Spanish villa. It was me but from the year 2000. Chirpily smiling back with squinted eyes, was my ten-year-old self.

She wore a bandana in her hair and a yellow bikini top with swimming trunks. Freckles clustered over her cheeks while peeling red skin hid them from her nose. Her hair was almost white, maybe from the sun, but with age too. And suddenly her face dropped. Her cheeks turned the same red as her nose and her mouth opened in fear. Her dread filled me too. Her bone-straight, white chops of hair hid her face as she looked down towards her exposed stomach, then back to my eyes through the mirror. She pointed, hand stretched, at my stomach.

I looked down: slowly curdling through a perfectly round hole in the centre of my stomach were my innards. Churning out like ground meat in a butcher's sausage stuffer. It was as if some external hoover was silently, invisibly forcing everything and anything from the hole. I felt it like you sometimes did after drinking too much water, trickling down inside the mechanics of your body. And then the heat returned around my swelling feet that were planted firmly against the orange tiles of the bathroom. They'd now turned warm from my hot soles. I looked up. My reflection was laughing. Malice she was, vulgarly forcing her hands into the hole, pulling and ripping at her body. At *my* body.

I knew she was doing this to me, invisibly ripping everything from inside. And just as I tried to speak to her I was gone. There was darkness.

Two rings, silence. Two rings, silence -

"Koral?"
So, she still called me that.

"Tilda."
"Long time."
There's a reason why.
"Yeah, listen. If Wester's around could I come by?" I wanted to be quick, we'd grown apart and I didn't want tedious small talk.
Truth be told, the girl I'd spent my childhood with, I didn't think I liked much now. Except for her enabling of this favour.
"Yeah, I guess." She paused, "Are you ok?"
As if you care
"Yeah, yeah." My voice high pitched, "Just got a lot of events and stuff. Don't trust anyone else." I tried to sound casual. It worked, I thought as I left her house with a bag of cocaine from her boyfriend less than an hour later.

——

Was I naive in thinking
that your love was like a drug
when I had never done them before
was I foolish to think
that I was smart
because it turned out to be better

——

In illness we crave
comfort in words
or warmth from a loved one
mother asking what you want for tea
while you're lying with
blankets on the sofa
so you'd never touch the leather
daytime tv boring your way until
the house was filled once more
3 pm onwards
but when they're gone
you seek it in nostalgia
those things you used to eat and drink
food before food became a thought
cream soda
when the only thing you wondered was how
they got the flavour like that
not how much sugar
could possibly be in a pack
so in illness I crave nostalgia
I let it consume me
and think like a placebo
that it has made me better
now my body is refilled with X, Y & Z
until I have to try again
with the fruits of our time

The weekend stop at the corner store
on the country ride
a single track wind
over field and moor
even more welcoming it was
for he unfortunate
to be in the middle seat this time
two days
Toy Story 2
Shrek 1
and 2
that giraffe ride at the pub
pool and Diet Cokes
water for me
I didn't like fizzy pop then
coco puffs
chips with ketchup
lots of ketchup
ketchup with everything
sausages in square shaped burgers
throwing up blood and meat in the bath tub

- X, Y & Z

The Beautiful Interpretational Taboo On Drugs

—

I got full marks
but liked being dumb
I punched and kicked
but still felt numb
I missed your calls
when I wanted your voice
blamed everyone else
when it was my choice
I painted cries with laughter
until both ran their course
I sobered myself up
to feel regret and remorse

—

I was a money maker for them. A piece to showcase and sell, send to events and interviews. All for their 30%. They rang and they rang and they rang. Opening at ten and closing at five, they sent emails and letters of congratulations on the film, reminded me of my potential and talent. I could see straight through them. *They didn't care*, I thought. They would care even less if they saw the spots that now dotted my face, the bags under my eyes and the drawn skin that now clung to my gaunt figure as if it were two sizes too small.

—

There's so much space in this cubicle
now I don't share
so much more space
space for her to stare
through the cracks of the door
prove it I thought
it's colder now
now there's not so many there
not so many hairs
not too many pounds
layering me where
now I wear
wear
worn

—

A part of me felt perpetually in their debt; they had made me. They had given me success and opportunities. Hell, I'd have never met Grace if it weren't for them. *Would that have been such a bad thing?*

I'd spent years begging. For auditions, recognition, for appreciation and love. *There is no love in the movie business*, my bitter self remarked. What they did give me, I now disregarded and threw away as if I'd lost all concept of value.

Fuck them. Fuck him. Fuck her.

No, fuck myself.

Months of not feeling anything. Not answering their calls because I didn't care what they thought of me. I didn't care about my life, why the hell would I care about my career? I lived for the pain of cocaine, through to the back of my left eye it would go, and the numbing it gave after. I would take more until I feared I'd taken too much and have a panic attack. Or I would take more when the withdrawal shakes and tensing came, prolonging the comedown, but only feeding it for a bigger fight with my body later. Why? Because then I would *feel.*

When I ran out of cocaine I would bleach my hair. But before anything I threw away the gloves - that's the point. I shook and squeezed from the bottle to my hand, massaging it around the roots of my hair. I would rub my hands together, layer by layer, until a white rash formed over my palms - usually about ten minutes. That's when the tingling would start. *The sting, the burn.* The first time it happened, it was an accident, and I was so submerged in fear that I rang the emergency doctor. Though, as soon as I realised I wasn't going to die I hung up, dried my hair with a stinging grip to the dryer, and started to see fragments of my younger self with each strand of lightened hair that dried - the only thing that still reminded me of that girl, and it was artificial.

Then with most things like this, I started to enjoy it. Blisters would form, I'd pick them, testing my pain threshold, allowing it to grow like my body's tolerance for drugs. Then I would forget for a while, maybe begin to wash the mounting pile of dishes in my apartment to pass the time and feel *real* pain. The heat and soap against my open wounds would force me to sit imperfectly and tarnished like those dishes, holding the damaged parts of my hands with tears in my eyes, red spilling from the cracks.

Cocaine and bleach did the same thing: adrenaline would course through my veins again just like when Grace's hand first touched mine back in Salt Lake or when Bryce would plant those kisses along my back whilst we watched *Hannibal Lector* films.

Shit, don't let me think of those times.

—

Every smile
a wasted step towards a wrinkle
every date
a wasted beat towards heartbreak
every hit
a step towards exuberance

—

Some would think I'm broken. That I'd fucked my life up. Some might look down on me now, maybe be reminded of the homeless getting their fix, or a rich girl of privilege enjoying the luxury of experimental drugs in her youth, unknowingly bought from her parent's pockets. Everyone wants to put me in a box somehow, a box they've assembled with their skewed opinions - *The beautiful interpretational taboo on drugs.* Well, I'll stay in the box if it means I don't have to think about anyone on the outside. Just me, myself and the box. How long will it take for claustrophobia to creep?

Some might hope I'd get better. Or even think that this was all just a phase and the next chapter in my life was recovery- as simple as that. Do those people know what it's like to replace love, conversations, everything you might hold value to in life with substance? Do they realise then, how important it becomes? How you question everything else in your life but the £80 leaving our account twice a week. I really didn't give a fuck what happened next. If this was a phase, I thought it would be a rather long one. I was numb. And that numbness was all I needed now. Numb from cocaine and bleach. But mostly from heartbreak. I think of it all and laugh. How weak was I to let love control me like that? *How weak are we all to put love in control of our actions?*

My favourite was him. And then her. And then *it.* Much smarter to be controlled by a thing brought to me in a little plastic bag every week by somebody who didn't care where it went as long as he got his money. I liked him, we weren't so different. Except he was led by money, and I by substance. We held a secret, the assumption of my state, which he happily kept safe from Tilda.

Eventually,

I would slip that special secret into my bag in exchange for bank notes. I would drain my account and fill my body. Then when my body was empty I'd slip into bed and fill it again: an empty deodorant bottle by my bed. Occasionally he or she might slip into my mind and I'd moan, and then cry myself to sleep.

—

A fuck for cola no
so I give him money
and watch him go
falling back into my sleigh
to see Florida snow
and fly higher
leaving happy trails
of cold icing
do you see how red my blood looks
against the white
it drops from where
my gold dust hides
the holes
in my nose
they're numb

- Keys to feel

—

Another course for the vain
course for the veins
coursing through the veins
to smooth the pain
but not the mind

dissolving
inside me
part of me

—

A Reflection

High vis and scaffolding couldn't fix me
nor fresh coats of paint
renovations to a bruised body
drilling into wrong places
plastering but leaving spaces
that would cause cracks to fall
sink and subside
but be rebuilt with growth
acceptance and time

I couldn't ease the frowns sinking deep into my forehead, nor the thoughts that accompanied them. To think of that time in my life came with ambivalence. It went by in a haze of smoke thicker than those cast by flares in the crowds of festivals. But where bright red and blue erupted from hands with canisters in the summer, only grey seemed to puff around my memories of those past few months spent alone.

I'm not sure what I really learned from addiction - other than not to do it again. I experienced the spiral down the slide. Where at first I glided, enjoying the highs of warm summer nights with a hum of distant music, but then plummeted around and around and around, and hit the bottom. Where dirt and rainwater sat as it would in a pond, mouldered. And my friends saw me from the top of the slide, saw how I had landed, my body sodden, and decided not to follow. I got through it though. I dried my body, escaped the static cling from the friction of the slide. And now, here I found myself sitting in reflection, never wanting to visit the park again, with a small part of myself resenting my parents for their lack of support, for allowing me to play on the park without their shadowing.

I understood why they weren't there for me; when someone you love is suffering, it's easier to leave, not watch them destroy themselves. Better to forget about them than to feel their pain alongside your own guilt for being unable to save them. But I couldn't be saved, not until I chose to change myself. Addiction cannot be beaten in the presence of adamance and reluctance. I had to see that destroying my body was not fashionable. I had to see that glazing over my cracks with cocaine would not cement them shut. My vision had been tinted with glasses of freedom. And I took that freedom too far, with nobody by my side to govern my usage. No judgement for replacing a meal with powder. And no care for myself—after my heart had given its all to others—I was drained of any emotion that could have been used to sway me from the bad stuff.

I always knew I was susceptible to addiction. I'd coasted through adult life naively thinking like a teenager, that drugs made the people at festivals more affluent, hierarchical. I grew apart from friends who moaned about substance abuse, as I sat in silence with my sniggering thoughts that I had better, more famous friends, musicians I knew - the ones who gave me my first taste for the high. *Oh, how much better my life is. If only you didn't live such a sheltered way—if you just* lived *a little. Maybe you could escape your mundane, recurring, moans of your nine to five job and desperate need for the weekend. Escape with a little of this substance you rage against.*

Our opposing views became so prominent, I locked them out along with my family, with everyone else.

I did go back to my parents eventually though. I was scarred, but having found the ability to rehabilitate myself, I soon found that I never needed a replacement at all. For so long I had spent my days trying to replace the loves of my life with *something* that I never gave time to see if the cracks would heal on their own. Acceptance was all it took. Once I did that I could accept love from others again. I accepted myself as a person. Not as half of something that thrived only upon completion by another. I practised my hobbies and found self-love in my talents. I bought a guitar but decided to skip over the minor detail that it bore a slight resemblance to Bryce's. But I played differently, not as good, but in my own way. I wrote my own way. I was authentically, and finally, unapologetically myself, with little accents of those who'd left their mark on me seeping through the scarring. The scarring that didn't hurt me anymore, but was still visible. The scarring I'd stopped trying to cover with *things* and instead accepted, regardless of whether it ever did heal.

I told my family I loved them and that I was sorry. I realised they found it too difficult to speak about still. Though my eyes had finally lost their blueish tone beneath, and my skeleton no longer protruded so much, my mother could still see the remains. Strain emitted pauses in her speech, the waving of her hands replacing nouns too difficult to voice. She reminded me that she worried about me now, more than she ever had done before, whilst hurriedly cooking dinner on my first visit back:

She worried now

more than when I
was late home
before she thought
the sky grew dark
and I was too young
to be out alone

more than when I
convinced her
that I was fine on my own
then plummeted
down the slopes
making dents in the snow
and other skiers slow

more than when I
cried
because the children laughed
at the colour of my hair
and the freckles on my skin

she worried

—

Blacking out in a daydream of
doing it on the kitchen marble top
while mother slept in bed
breaking it up with the kitchen spoon
the same one I used
to make her a brew
I'm not breathing
an inhale brings me back
when she walks through
and sees
it's still what I want
at least
it's no longer
between my fingers
every time I pick up the phone
beneath the case
would there be sat
the deadly sacrifice
asking to perfume my nose
every time my fingers
ran over the grooves of the bag
it's good
because now
I can smell the tea
taste the tea
with occasional toxic daydreams
is what I will do
to see the nights clean
with you
mum

—

Eventually,

part three
the breakthrough

Eventually,

Poseidon

An abandoned platform
peeling paint
dusting rails
no room to wait
a daunting feeling
seeing fate
my one way ticket
has a date
the wheels are hard
against the track
it stops at the platform
no going back
my train has stopped
with me alone
and in the platform
a telephone
as shrill as laughter
as sad as death
the sound of rings
takes my breath
and as I listen
words weigh a tonne
I know it's not long
until I'm gone

I walked towards the double doors of the church. Anticipation played on my heart like a fiddle, amplifying through my chest and around my ears; it made me hesitate before knocking. I wiggled my toes into the gravel and heard that familiar crunch beneath my feet. I saw no movement through the stained glass windows of each wooden door. A small part of me was glad, too nervous to confront him. But a bigger part of me needed him to know that it hadn't worked out with Grace. That maybe I was always better suited to him. I knew it was selfish of me to be here. I knew how hard it must have been for him to heal, and I really didn't want to break that or take him two steps back by seeing me now, but I guess selfishness was a trait I would never steer too far from. And would he have to take any steps back if he accepted me again?

I saw my reflection as I contemplated whether or not to turn and leave. After seeing my body contort into a skeleton; after my complexion had grown more peaky and pale; I saw that I now looked the same as I had before it all. I never thought I could like myself again, but here I stood reminded of my old self, prided with red and blue glass that would outlive god knows how many relationships within the wall before me. I only held hope that tonight, they would see reconciliation. Everything could be perfect again, with those stained glass windows onlooking the rest of our forever.

—

I overthink
to compensate
for the time
I didn't at all

—

Eventually,

—

Crash into me
drench me
flood me
drown me
with your love
for I never want to be dry
if it means
a life
without you
scold me with the back of the spoon
mark me as your own
carve me like a pig
engrave your initials upon me
to remind me everyday
of how much I enjoy the pain
like the needle of a tattoo
but instead of ink
give me your touch
give me your breath
give me everything
you can give
that's free

—

A light flickered on to my right. It lit a box across the garden, but left me in the shadows, unseen. I crept closer, craving a glimpse of him. I don't know what I expected to see, but what awaited my eyes beclouded my head more than three consecutive cigarettes. Anger rose inside me so fast I painted a sickening master piece in my mind of his life after us - painted with foul colours. I had to turn away. The longer I looked, the more menacing it would become, his own portrait of *Dorian Gray*. Except this one showed two. And the girl sat beside him on the sofa was unmistakably familiar, and even more menacing.

Tilda.

—

He was my world my water my sea
he wove his words for me
then moved his tide
and now
their words swam lengths
I imagined the sounds they would make
bouncing from the ceiling
rippling echoes
while all I could hear
was words of thistle and wind
talking loudly behind
their words dry
his legs curled with laughter
her body flirting faster
a stroke of his cheek
a smile from the sea
and I was gone

- Tident

—

I had always thought things happened for a reason. But sitting in my car, driving home with tears endlessly flowing, I really didn't think there would ever be a silver lining to this. I couldn't even say their names. Seeing them together was enough as if saying their names out loud, or even in my head, would solidify what I saw. But I know what I saw. I knew that touch all too well to know it wasn't just platonic. I hadn't spoken to Tilda since turning up at her house for drugs, which I was sure she'd have told Bryce about. So instead of a storm that made me appreciate the warmth after, this was an earthquake. Where people died and couldn't feel the heat after - because they were dead.

——

It took everything in my willpower that night
not to lean my hands to the right
and crash into the metal railing
and the darkness beyond
it took everything
not to hit my head against the wheel
or speed past the policemen scattered around the A15
so they could stop me
give me a distraction from being
wheel deep in a blind summit
open cans by my side
never straying from my mind
like the speedometer getting higher
marginally speeding at 75
80
85…

——

——

There's not really any songs I can listen to
to make me feel better
no serenity in my silence
no force that could halt my speed in time
if others should come to the road
testing my sobriety
with words from sirens
oh the exhilaration
when that car door opened
giving me a taste
for the rush of it again
don't go back don't go back
look what happens
if you go back

——

Three hours later my bags lay neatly packed on my unmade bed, as ready as I. I knew what I was going to do. Seeing everything tonight had guided my mind in the right direction after all. And I was gone.

Leaving Brightside

I had always hated airport queues. I was wearing a floor length faux fur coat. Bright emerald. That probably didn't help. People stared a little too long, even after I met their eyes with mine. I'm sure one woman whispered my name to her husband but I pretended not to hear. I hoped today that half of them might not have known who I was. I didn't want the attention or hassle of talking to strangers who recognised me, or taking pictures with the ones who did, on less than four hours sleep. I had landed in LA. I was ready to apologise for my actions, and own up to my stupidity and just get back to what I had always loved the most: acting.

I never understood why airport staff were so rude. I smiled at each one in an attempt to find a mutual kindness, with little success. I waited behind the red line until called forward with only a hand gesture and a grunt. He gave me lotion and wiped my hands after numerous attempts at scanning my fingerprint.

I still had blisters so worn into my skin from the months of bleach that my fingerprints were unrecognisable. I finally got through passport control after speaking to a slightly more understanding officer, who took me into his office and asked me questions about the nature of my visit and how my hands came to be so ruined. He said I reminded him of his daughter, giving me a little guilt as I thought of my own parents. He told me to look after myself and ushered me away, with a comforting smile which filled me with happiness, towards the airport exit.

I smiled at the sun that greeted me from the sliding doors of the airport. I winced at the smell of cigarettes and car fumes. I was finally here. Not Salt Lake, nor Vegas, or the church, but a place where I was good. I think I was happier at that moment, even after everything, because I was good. And that was all I needed.

Hello, sweet second chances…

——

Relax

let the light guide you
like it did before
the pain will be temporary
and will soon be a memory
that will allow you later
to appreciate laughter
and accept happiness

relax

——

At Last

Etta James was playing on the radio from the kitchen. I had turned the volume down when last inside to collect snacks, so it was now only a hum in the background. I was lying in my garden, scattering the grass around me with orange peel. Closing my eyes, I let the sun warm my eyelids, the music lulled me with calm. For the first in what felt like forever, I laughed. No reason. *Did I need one?*

I used to think that maybe in years to come, with wrinkles hugging my lips from the years of progressive smoking, I'd be crying over another person I'd fallen in love with. Maybe I laugh because now I know there will never be anyone quite like Bryce -or Grace. I know I will never fall in love quite like that again and I'm ok with that. I'm ok with my thoughts for company. Once I'd arranged the mess inside my head I actually found it to be quite a nice place to be.

Of course, silence isn't always my best friend, but for those time there's the music. I no longer dread the time for sleep, dread when the confrontation our minds must face when there are no distractions or escapes from our thoughts. I no longer rely on others or have to use the future as a pretence to fooling myself into happiness. I need not think of the future and what it might hold to get me through the *now*. Because finally, my happiness was now, not something distant, something that I held hope would come soon.

I guess that was my way of dealing with things after abusing my body: news articles, films, books, music, parties, conversations and events. And they were great. They made me genuinely happy - until I was alone again. I soon realised they couldn't be my only source of happiness, nor anyone else's. They helped, they were a stepping stone away from abuse, but they were not the answer.

For loneliness creeps on us all at some point: a train ride when we forget our headphones, when your phone loses battery, those silent moments before sleep. And what of those times when we are truly alone? Loneliness should not be inherently linked to sadness. Loneliness can be bliss if only you can face the thoughts that eventually catch up with you, the ones you can't run from. They can be deadly. They might even be killing you now, subconsciously, allowing you to cling to those external sources of happiness so dearly without realising the extremity of your reliance for them. *So*, I thought, *let them catch up with you. Stare them right in the face. If you don't, they will kill you. Kill you as much as if you were still filling your body with substance and cigarettes.*

But know that you can kill them too. So beat them to it. Kill them and enjoy the company of your thoughts that might one day fester an idea, a whole new life, a song, a book, a scientific discovery. Your mind can kill you, but it can do a damned good job of accompanying you through some of the best moments in life, alone.

I quit smoking too, which I guess is my happy ending. I quit because I felt like I was cheating myself. How could I say I was sober but smoke a cigarette to get a rush from the nicotine? I found what I think must be *closure* in quitting those cigarettes Bryce introduced me to - I thought it was about time anyway, considering I had always ticked the 'non-smoker' box on health questionnaires.

'And here we are in heaven'

Bryce was right; Those three months were the best of my life. Equal only to the years we'd spent together before. But I was right too; they were hard. The ultimatum of choosing who I loved more. The impossible task of hurting nobody and coming out unscratched myself.

The two were incomparable. To do so would be an insult; I didn't choose Grace because she was better than him. Sometimes you just do things you can't explain. Because at the time it feels right.

I no longer think of myself as a bad person, having fallen for two people at once. I no longer allow guilt to ride my thoughts like an adrenaline junkie at a theme park. Best of all, I've found contentment with being alone. I now look back at those times in my life as fond memories, not heartbreak and regret, no squirming stomach to accompany the nostalgia of two people that I fell madly in love with. To both I thank, I love, and would give my life for, still. We don't speak anymore. But I'm ok with that.

I'm still learning to listen to his music without blacking out in a nostalgic daydream. And mostly now, when his songs are played on the radio, I'm filled with nothing but pride. I feel lucky to have known him. I'm glad at least the music wasn't ruined by my actions. That was always important to me.

I listened to Tame Impala's first album too. It wasn't the same as *that* one, but it's often played on long drives through the countryside, where I now live. It might flicker a remembrance to our hands touching on the gear stick, or the colour of the octagonal patterned carpets that witnessed our first kiss - the moment I realised my life would be turned upside down by my second love. I'll welcome those thoughts now, and easily let them pass again when the song ends. And eventually, I'm happy. Because I got to know them both. And shared something I never knew existed until then.

What am I in love with, if not for some*one*? I've fallen in love with freedom, the sun on my skin and the orange circles it casts over my eyes. The way it stays longer with each week, telling me Spring is ending, Summer beginning. Freedom: where there's a whistling wind that silences sound from my ears when I cycle down narrowing roads, nothing but hills in sight.

And on the top of a hill stands an old church, just visible in the evening light. Where often you can see ambers of light from the windows. I sometimes wonder what he is doing inside. I do hope he's kept the parts of me etched into the walls. That he hasn't painted over our memories with magnolia, but instead, has found someone to complement them. I hope he loves them as much as he had loved me and I hope that whoever they are, they will never fall in love with another person and break his heart like I had. I hope he thinks of me every now and then and looks back to the start of our days in the church, or the day we met in the mud and cold of a festival. I hope he smiles.

Cycling, my thighs burn, snot seeps from my nose and my throat becomes too dry when the last drops of water fall from the bottle to my mouth. And soon enough, the brow of the hill will pass my wheels and feeling will regain. The pain will fade and at the end of each ride I feel glad I did it. Glad I endured the pain to feel the pure ecstasy of riding down the hills.

It's all worth it,

Eventually.

Eventually,

The End

About The Author

Emma Laird is an English actress, model and writer. Funnily enough, she was scouted at a music festival back in 2013 and has since spent six years in the fashion industry working with the likes of Valentino, Vogue, Grazia, Glamour and Louis Vuitton to name a few.

With thanks to her mother agency, Models 1, Emma has worked across the world, from Tokyo to Sydney, and many places in between. While working in New York, she enrolled at New York Film Academy to study Acting for Television & Film and has since continued her studies back in London to further her career in the film industry. Emma is currently seeing her latest film, which she won her first award for Best Actress, circulate film festivals globally.

Growing up in Peak District, Emma now lives just outside of London, but makes regular trips back to the countryside in her trusty Jeep.

Eventually, is Emma's first novel.

Red Dagon

The cover was black and white, a girl's back curved, a shade in between each rib. I flipped it over and read the track list. Curious of whether he wrote better after heartbreak, eager to find a trace of him amongst the titles.

1. the credits
2. leather clad
3. would you have?
4. on film she stays
5. dangerous nights
6. vale
7. dancing to rock
8. yesterday
9. in passing, I smile

How many were about me? Most of the songs could have been about anything. But *Dancing To Rock* made me smile and think of that night he watched me dance to Joy Division. My favourite memory.

I lingered on *In Passing, I Smile* hoping this was his message of forgiveness. That even if I didn't listen to the album, the title was his message. Almost as if he knew that I would read this. That I would be here, so self-absorbed to know that the songs were about me. I put it back on the shelf at the top, in front of a Tame Impala CD. I hoped it did well. I left the store with a Thomas Harris book and a smile on my face.

—

In the search for happiness
I lost love
in the search for peace
I found chaos
in the end
it worked out

—

spinning skinny
in your leather clad you
could be the one to set me free
and just like that you
could flee
but dancing to rock I watched
the girl I loved swirl and knot
her hands around mine
to have you in my arms oh
to relive that night

The Touch Of An Arm, She'd Have You Hooked

I saw her youth in front of me
her golden ringlets
that swayed with clumsiness
her animation
brought to life by affection
from those who shared
her sweet disposition

masking wrinkles
sat a smile of distraction
it made me think of warmth and gold
oh how could you
grow old
of her charm
her laughter
her loudness
her lack of care
for what others thought
if they heard her speak
because her words caught by strangers
would sit on their mantlepieces
they would tear away cherished memories
if only to know
how to create more with her

and even now her youth infected me
through pictures it poured
though her voice over a call
I saw it in all forms
and despised it all

My sourness towards her wrinkled my nose. I hated to admit it but I think I always knew - what a friend I was. I knew her the most out of anyone, and then she met him and he changed her so easily. And nobody else saw it. How could nobody else see it? How fickle. How desperate she must have been to let somebody mould her, shape her, put words in her mouth and puppet her around like something he owned. I still called her by the name only I knew her by, but it didn't work. Saliva would build around my mouth that I would have to spit out, sour. That phone call had been hard. Like her electricity had been cut, she mumbled, sounded foreign and forced, asking for the one thing I knew would make her worse - I jumped at the chance. I made myself sick.

So I blocked her out. Just as she had done with me when she and Bryce had first found love.

And the worst part? I didn't even like him.

Nor he I.

- Tilda

Eventually,

Help

Drug addiction is touched upon in this book. There were many moments of questioning whether to include this part of my writing in the book for fear of sensationalising drug use. Ultimately Tilda's drug addiction is something I thought needed to be included for the narrative of the story, and the development of her character and personality.
Seeking help takes a lot of strength and courage. Please, if you're reading this and are struggling, or have been triggered, know that you are not alone and there is never any shame in seeking help, only strength..
Should you have been affected and need help, please use the resources below and/or seek help from your doctor.

https://www.nhs.uk/live-well/healthy-body/drug-addiction-getting-help/

Find details of local and national services that provide counselling and treatment in England by visiting this website:

https://www.talktofrank.com/get-help/find-support-near-you

HELPLINE: Frank drugs helpline 0300 123 6600

FOR INFORMATION ON DRUGS: Visit DrugWise to find out more information about drugs, alcohol and tobacco. Formerly DrugScope, DrugWise provides access to evidence-based drug, alcohol and tobacco information and resources, including an international knowledge hub.

Printed in Great Britain
by Amazon